Wake Up, Sleeping Beauty

Wake Up, Sleeping Beauty

June Fellhauer

Library of Congress Control Number:		2010906059
ISBN:	Hardcover	978-1-4500-9096-4
	Softcover	978-1-4500-9095-7
	Ebook	978-1-4500-9097-1

This book was printed in the United States of America.

To order additional copies of this book, contact:
Xlibris Corporation
1-888-795-4274
www.Xlibris.com
Orders@Xlibris.com
80359

Contents

Introduction

Living in a mortuary was never part of my dream!

When I was a little girl, I often went to my friend's house where we played for hours with her Dawn Dolls. These dolls were like miniature Barbies, and my friend had the complete collection, along with all the accessories.

I lived vicariously through these dolls. I wanted to grow up and have the perfect two-story house with the white picket fence, beautiful clothes, perfect children, and oh yes, the drop-dead gorgeous husband.

I set my idealistic plans. However, the choices I was making then were not leading me down the road to the "happily ever after" lifestyle. You see I was conducting my life according to the world's standards.

At the age of eighteen I found myself married with a baby girl, living in a mortuary. My husband, Jay, and I were desperate for money, so we moved into an old three-story, Victorian-style house that had been transformed into the town's mortuary. It was free rent if we answered the phone and kept the place clean. We also earned extra money if we sang for funerals and helped out the mortician. Jay and I could harmonize on "When the Roll is Called Up Yonder" like few others.

Every Thursday night, while Jay was away working another job, I was required to close the mortuary down for the night. The last two duties on the list were to close the casket (with the dead body in it) and turn off the lights. I remember the first time like it was yesterday. I slowly made my way down the aisle of the chapel, knowing that at the end waited a dead person who needed to be "shut in" for the night. I took a deep breath as I approached the casket. Quietly, slowly, I closed the upper half of the casket, hoping the body within it wouldn't suddenly open his eyes and spring back to life! Then, without taking my eyes off the casket, I reached for the lamp that illuminated the room. My fingers fumbled as they searched for the little black control. I took a deep breath and turned the switch; the room became black as a dungeon. I raced down the aisle, like an escaping prisoner. A sharp left turn at the end of the aisle and I was sprinting toward the stairs to the tower (our apartment). I leaped up the stairs, three at a time, darted through the living room and kitchen until I reached the sofa in the family room where our four-month-old daughter lay sleeping peacefully. I sat next to that sleeping baby, my heart pounding so loudly that my eardrums felt like they would explode. I waited, barely breathing, so I could hear every sound until my husband returned home at around midnight.

"I would never live in a mortuary!" you might say. It's a scary thought. I never pictured myself living there either. But in a sense, all of us have lived or are living in a "mortuary." The apostle Paul tells us that we are or were all dead in our sins because we have walked according to the ways of this world. We followed Satan, the "prince" of the power of the air (Ephesians 2:1-2). He has put a curse on us and wants us to remain dead in the darkness of his dungeon, oblivious to God's great plan for our life. He doesn't want us to know how fabulous God intends our lives to be.

Walking in sin imprisoned me in the mortuary—the darkness. But learning the ways of God helped me escape.

No longer am I a peasant living in a mortuary but the bride of "Prince Charming" better known as Jay, who after 29 years of marriage is still drop-dead gorgeous to me. I'm the queen of four beautiful princesses: Jolene, Jacque, Jerrilyn, and Jordan; and the queen-in-law to three wonderful sons: Jeffrey, Charlie, and Brandon. As you can see, everyone's name in the immediate Fellhauer family begins with the letter "J" and if you stay too long at our palace you, too, will have a name that begins with letter "J." Just ask my niece Jillary; her name use to be Hillary.

Serving as innkeeper to many teenage girls, and the stable keeper to a few horses, goats, Boston terriers, and our Rottweiler, Dolli, is a joy to me. My life is most blessed when those around me learn to walk in the ways of the kingdom.

I write this book with hopes that girls of every age will learn to recognize their Prince, be set free from the ways of the world, and live "happily ever after" in the promise land that God intended for her to live.

One of my favorite fairy tales is *Sleeping Beauty.* It's the one where baby Aurora is whisked into the forest to be raised by three good fairies who are trying to keep her from an evil fairy's curse. If Aurora touches the spindle of a spinning wheel before her sixteenth birthday, she will fall into a deep sleep and will never awaken unless she receives true love's kiss.

On the day of her sixteenth birthday, Aurora ventures into the forest by herself where she meets a stranger and falls in love. She doesn't know his name, much less that he is the prince who will one day save her from an evil curse.

When Aurora returns to the cottage, the three little fairies have a huge birthday surprise for her. She learns that she is a princess and must return to the palace to marry a prince that her parents have betrothed her to at an early age.

Sadly the princess is escorted back to the palace, thinking only about the love she has for the stranger in the woods. When they reach the palace, the fairies leave Aurora alone while they go to find her parents. A strange glow suddenly appears. In a trance, the princess follows the light to a room with a spinning wheel in it. Maleficent, the evil fairy, is in the room. "Touch the spindle!" Maleficent demands. Powerless, the princess obeys and the curse is put into motion. The young princess falls to the ground in a deep sleep.

Knowing that the stranger in the woods, Prince Phillip, is the only one who can deliver true love's kiss, Maleficent captures him and puts him in a dungeon.

The three little fairies come to Phillip's aid and set him free. They give him a shield of virtue and a sword of truth to help him defeat Maleficent.

Maleficent turns herself into a fire-breathing dragon and goes after the young prince. Phillip uses the shield to deflect her fiery flames and then plunges his sword into her heart, sending her over a cliff to her death.

Phillip makes his way back to the tower of the palace where he finds his love in a deep sleep. Lovingly, he leans over and kisses her with true love's kiss. The princess wakes and they live "happily ever after."

Little girls dream of becoming a princess and marrying the perfect prince, but do fairy tales really come true? They do if we learn how to detect true love's kiss and walk in the ways of God's kingdom. I will help you find the Prince that will gently awaken you with His kiss of love, desire, and deliverance. A Prince who will protect you, provide for you, and give you great pleasure. His kiss will bring you into the palace and invite you to share an extraordinary life.

Your life's story, your fairy tale, is just beginning. Are you ready to open up the fairy tale that the God of the universe has written for you and let yourself see how your dreams can come true?

The Bible calls it *Song of Songs* or *Song of Solomon*. God used King Solomon, the wealthiest and wisest king the world has ever known, to be His author. As we explore the *Song of Solomon* we will witness a loving relationship from the beginning stages of dating to the actual wedding night. We will learn and see through the eyes of God what a true prince looks like, what a prince desires from a woman, and how God intended sex and romance to be as we watch a couple make love on their wedding night.

Although it seems like a fairy tale, it actually happens to real people, and it really is true! It is about a real peasant girl who finds a real prince. It's about you finding your prince. I present to you, *Wake Up Sleeping Beauty*!

Chapter One

Kiss Me!

"May he kiss me with the kisses of his mouth!"
Song of Solomon 1:2

"Now the king of Israel, King David, was old, advanced in age; and they covered him with clothes, but he could not keep warm" (1King 1:1). Israel's king was dying and his sons were fighting for the throne. Prince Solomon's mother, Bathsheba, pleaded before the king, "You promised to put Prince Solomon on the throne."

All eyes of Israel were on King David as he made the final decision. "Call for Bathsheba," he ordered. The king vowed, "As the Lord lives who has redeemed my life from all distress, surely as I vowed to you by the Lord the God of Israel, saying, 'Your son Solomon shall be king after me, and he shall sit on my throne in my place; I will indeed do so this day'" (1 Kings 1:28-30).

Fast-forward several years . . .

A young Shulammite girl, somewhere between the ages of fourteen and seventeen, is working in the kingdom's vineyard. Sweat is pouring off of her brow as she dreams of an easier life. A commotion stirs in the street, people crowd to see the great parade. Could it be the young Prince Solomon, who every young girl dreamed about and who has now become the king? Gazing longingly into the cloudless Jerusalem sky, the Shulammite girl imagines her lips upon King Solomon's.

Do you remember your first kiss, or dream about being kissed for the very first time?

I sure remember mine. It was a cool spring evening. My friend and I were walking home from a junior high dance with her boyfriend and one of his friends. I knew the boys very well. In fact I had a crush on the friend, so I was thrilled that they were walking us home. As we got closer to my house, things seemed a little uncomfortable. How was the night going to end? Should I leave my friend alone with these two guys? Would she kiss her boyfriend good night? I dreamed about kissing his friend. Oh, the questions and the situations that were popping into my mind!

We were standing at my back door when it happened. My friend's boyfriend kissed her!

I'm not sure if it was out of panic or machoism, but before I knew it, the friend kissed me too! I wasn't ready for it. I was expecting a peck on the cheek or maybe even a gentle kiss on the lips, but this kiss was more like when the doctor puts one of those long wooden tongue depressors in your mouth and then swabs your tonsils; causing your gag reflexes to take over! I nearly hurled. Yes, at thirteen this kiss was the worst thing I had ever experienced. My kissing days were over.

Thank goodness I overcame my fear and dislike of kissing. Had I never kissed again I would never have had the passionate moments that I have had with my husband for the past twenty-five years. You might be saying, "Stop!" This is too much information!" But the truth is that I would have missed out on some of the most romantic and incredible times of my life. I'm really glad that my first experience with kissing wasn't the true picture of kissing.

Kissing has been around since the beginning of man. God has been using the simple kiss as a way for us to show affection for generations, but did you know that He also uses it as a tool for us to discover a good prince from a bad one?

The Shulammite dreams about Solomon, a young prince who has just become the king of Israel. After all he is the wisest, wealthiest man the world has ever known. He's a man who could promise her protection, provision, and pleasure. I imagine, she dreams about him valiantly fighting for her honor, killing wild game to nourish her, and romantically drawing her into his body and making love to her all night long. She longs for a man to provide for her, give her security, and love her "until death do them part."

It's the kind of love that fairy tales are made of and it all starts with dreaming about his kisses.

She wants his kisses (plural), as she knows that there is more than one kind of kiss. In her native Hebrew language the word for kiss is *nashaq*. It's pronounced *naw-shak* and means to touch or fasten up. When our lips touch or fasten to someone else's lips we are *nashaqing*. The Scriptures tell us that there are four different kinds of *nashaq*; three that we will all strongly desire and the fourth we will spend the rest of our lives trying to avoid. The kisses we desire are *phileo*, *chashaq,* and *nasaq*. Each is a gift from God and has an appropriate place and time to be used.

Peaches, prunes, and alfalfa were the words we used to describe the different kinds of kisses when I was in junior high. My friends and I would make our lips really tight as we said "peaches," we would pucker up our lips as we said "prunes," and, well, when we said "alfalfa" our tongues licked out with each syllable. Disgusting, I know, but each kiss represented a different level of the relationship.

The kiss of peaches was given when you were first dating someone and a bit on the shy side. It was usually a peck on the check. The kiss of prunes was used for the more serious dater and was a romantic kiss on the lips. The kiss of alfalfa, well, let's just say that according to us (me and my girl friends) good girls never gave it or received it. We knew, or thought we knew, how serious our friends were about their boyfriends by the way they would let the boy kiss them. (Of course, this theory got thrown out the window when I received my first kiss.)

It's funny to me because God is actually using physical kisses to show us what is going on in the spiritual (in our hearts). His kisses are for our enjoyment and pleasure but each kiss comes with boundaries and instructions. If we follow the instructions we will know what kind of a guy we are dating by the kind of kisses he offers us.

The first kiss that the Shulammite girl dreams of is the kiss of *phileo*. In Greek it means to "be a friend." This kiss is a way of greeting each other and shows brotherly or sisterly love. It is usually given on the cheek to show favor. It's something that our souls desire. We all want someone to befriend us, someone we can share things with and trust. It shows that we are a part of something, a family or a group of friends that share a common interest. The apostle Paul told believers to "greet one another with a holy [*phileo*] kiss" (I Corinthians 16:24). This kiss can come in the form of a friendly hug, an encouraging word, a firm handshake, or just a look of acceptance.

Our souls were created to crave the kiss of friendship because we were never created to be alone.

Imagine the Shulammite girl as she brushes her thick black hair from her smudged, tired face—melting within—as Solomon extends his hand to her to help her up from the dusty floor of the vineyard and offers her with a cool drink of water. She tingles inside as she receives her first kiss of *phileo.*

The kiss of *phileo* is the kiss of friendship; it is used for dating and can be compared to "peaches."

The second kiss that she will long for is the kiss of *chashaq* (khaw-shak), which means, "cling to, to love, to deliver, to have a desire and delight in." This is not a passionate, throw-you-down-in-the-hay kind of kiss. It's a warm, deep, gentle "I love you" kiss; a kiss where no words are needed. She dreams about someone loving her and delivering her from the dungeon of the vineyard. She knows that this kind of kiss isn't freely available because, in the days of Solomon, kissing the opposite sex in public was strictly forbidden unless it was a sibling. Kissing in school halls would have been against the law, for sure!

"This kiss, his love, is better than wine," she says. It's stronger than words. It changes lives. It's the kiss of "love" and she dreams of the prince that she can cling to, the one who will love her, deliver her, and respect her. Our hearts dream about this kiss. We dream about receiving it from a prince who adores us, cherishes us, says great thing about us. We envision a devoted, committed prince bowing down before us on one knee and asking us to be his bride.

The kiss of *chashaq* is for two hearts committed to each other: Two people who can't stand to be apart, delight in each other's company, defend each other and fight for each other's honor and respect. *Chashaq* requires commitment; it represents prunes and is to be saved and used for engagement. I'm not telling you that it's wrong to kiss someone on the lips before being engaged; I'm cautioning you to check your heart and motives. Remember, God is trying to show us in the physical what is going on in the spiritual (heart).

Who is that man out there who can deliver us from our troubles, give us respect, and meet our desires? We search franticly for him. We keep kissing, kissing, kissing, trying to find "Mr. Right," to no avail. There is danger in this because the root word of *nashaq* is *nasaq* pronounced *"naw-sak"* and it means "to catch fire, burn, or kindle." *Nasaq* is so intimate that it will cause your body to become hot with passion. It is the third kiss that the Shulammite one-day desires.

Alfalfa is an understatement of this kiss. Television portrays this kiss as two people passionately kissing, undressing each other and eventually having sex. There's one problem: Television never has them get married first.

God ordained this kiss but with strict boundaries. Only where there is a commitment of protection, provision, and pleasure is this kiss to be used. Marriage—that's it! There is no other place for *nasaq*. When I received my first kiss was I sinning? No! My heart was nowhere near this kind of passion. Remember, God is trying to show us what is going on in the heart. I'm just trying to show you the elevated passion in these three physical kisses.

Let me explain these kisses as they were explained to me. You and your date are sitting on the couch enjoying hot chocolate. There's a warm fire burning in the fireplace. Things start to get a little cozy. This fire is creating an atmosphere of warmth and love. You begin to play "smacky-face." It all starts out innocently with the kiss of *phileo.* The warmth builds and before you know it you are in a horizontal position exchanging the kiss of *chashaq*. While you're not paying attention to what's going on around you, a spark flies out into the middle of the living room. Things are not only heating up in the room but in your body. Your flesh is longing for the passionate kiss of *nasaq*. The fire is completely out of control. It has no boundaries. The whole house is engulfed in flames. You are no longer passionate about your boyfriend, you are running for your life!

Phileo, chashaq, and *nasaq* are warm, loving, and exciting but can burn us if not used according to God's directions. When shared according to His ways, they are life-changing, exciting, and sensual, but when expressed outside of God's borders, they become combustible and dangerous.

Let's make sure we have a clear picture of what these kisses look like and where they are to be used.

Kisses
(*Nashaq*)

Dating	Engagement	Marriage
Phileo	*Chashaq*	*Nasaq*
(Our soul's desire)	(Our heart's desire)	(Our body's desire)
Friendship	**Love**	**Passion**
Sharing	Cling to	Burn
Trust	To Deliver	Kindle
Common Interest	Desire	Pleasure
Encouragement	Protect	Intimacy
Romance	Provision	Catch fire

Dear sweet girls, it's not wrong to want these kisses; in fact, we were created to desire them. But if we receive them out of their boundaries they will cause us great turmoil.

Solomon's people, the Israelites, were notorious for taking God's kisses out of their boundaries. But when they did, it caused them poverty, unwanted pregnancies, diseases, dysfunctional families, famines, and moral decline that led them into captivity.

At one point while in captivity the Israelites called out to God, "Please send us a Prince and deliver us from our sorrows." In other words, get us back within the correct boundaries; get us back to living life according to Your ways.

God in His mercy and grace sent a prophet named Isaiah to deliver a message to them: "For a child will be born to us, a son will be given to us; and the government will rest on His shoulder; and His name will be called Wonderful Counselor, Mighty God, Eternal Father, Prince of Peace" (Isaiah 9:6).

Most of the Israelites missed God because they were looking for some tall, dark, handsome warrior to fix all of their external problems. And the Prince of Peace came to fix their internal problems. He came to fix their souls knowing that the external would naturally follow.

Many of us are the same way; we are looking for some guy to come along and fix us and our problems when in fact, our wants are not external but internal.

God is trying to tell us if we want our physical life to be great and we want to have a great relationship with a great prince, then we must first pick a great spiritual Prince. May I introduce you to your two spiritual choices: (1) Jesus, Prince of Peace or (2) Satan, Prince of this World.

His Name is Jesus: Prince of Peace

He is the same Prince that the Israelites were looking for. He is the Prince of Peace. His name is Jesus. The Bible tells us that He existed in the beginning before the world was created. He is still alive today, and will continue to live forever. He was a physical prince and is a spiritual prince. No other prince is equal to Him, either in fairy tales or in real life. Jesus is God. How is it then that He understands our struggles? He—Almighty God—clothed His Spirit in human flesh and became as human as you and me. He walked this earth just like you and I do.

"I came," Jesus said, "That they may have life, and have it abundantly" (John 10:10, RSV). He came so that you might live "happily ever after."

Satan: Prince of this World

Who is Satan? He is an evil spiritual prince—best friend of the evil fairy Maleficent. "Satan . . . was a murderer from the beginning, not holding to the truth, for there is no truth in him. When he lies, he speaks his native language, for he is a liar and the father of lies" (John 8:44).

Sometimes it's hard to detect Satan and his lies because he was a "beautiful angel full of wisdom and perfect in beauty" (Ezekiel 28:12). What he has to say to you might sound really good to start with but will always be disastrous in the end. In Scripture you will see that he is called the "prince of this world" as well as "son of the morning," "prince of the power of the air," "Beelzebub," "Devil," "Belial." (John 12:31, James 4:7, 2 Cor. 6:15, Eph. 2:2)

Satan, like Maleficent, came to the party (earth) to kill, steal, and destroy us (John 10:10). He wants to inflict great pain, grief, and death upon us. He does this by taking every kiss that God has given us, the kiss of *phileo* (friendship), *chashaq* (love), and *nasaq* (passion) and distorts them, takes them out of their boundaries, and turns them upside down, giving us the kiss of (betrayal). It is the fourth kiss. Betrayal is the kiss that we want to avoid.

Kisses of Betrayal or Frogs
(Kisses Upside Down)
Nashaq

Phileo	*Chashaq*	*Nasaq*
Friendship—Enemy	**Love**—Hate	**Passion**—Lust
Sharing—Gossip	Cling To—Control	Burn—Pornography
Trust—Fear	Protect—Harm	Kindle—Homosexuality
Interest—Fatal Attraction	Desire—Detest	Pleasure—Pre-marital Sex
Encouragement—Insecurity	Deliver—Imprison	Intimacy—Many Lovers
Romance—Tragedy	Provision—Deprive	

Satan's goal is to give us kisses of betrayal so that the curses of death will fall upon us: Death of relationships, death of sexual purity, death of self-esteem, and death of self-control. Satan's ultimate kiss of betrayal—the kiss of eternal death—is to block you from knowing the "Prince of Peace" and from living eternally. Satan's greatest battlefield is our minds so he has devised three great resources in delivering his kisses: media, frogs, and people closest to us.

Media

By reading magazines and watching television ads, thoughts enter our minds like we aren't worthy enough, popular enough, skinny enough, pretty enough, smart enough; we don't deserve happiness; we won't receive happiness until we possess certain things; we will never measure up; and the list goes on. If we believe Satan's deceitful kisses, we will become very self-centered and very insecure. The death of self-esteem will hit us like a ton of bricks.

God's kisses say we are fearfully and wonderfully made, pure, righteous, beautiful, loved, anointed, set apart, powerful, able to overcome adversity, and much more (Ps. 139:14, Is. 61:10, Ps. 28:8, 1 John 2:27, 2 Cor. 1:21, Prov. 18:21, Acts 1:8, Eph. 3:20). If we believe, these kisses will become secure, and very powerful through Christ.

Frogs

Satan loves to use frogs to deliver his kisses. Frogs are: (1) Guys who say one thing and do another; (2) Guys who will convince you to take every kiss out of its appropriate boundary; (3) Guys who will flip the kisses upside down; (4) Guys who hop away from responsibility.

Frogs disappoint and trouble us. We think that they are giving us the kiss of friendship, but they turn out to be our worst enemy. They share our secrets, become our competitors, and leave us dumbfounded as they cheat on us when someone else comes along. Our common interest becomes fatal attraction as they isolate us from our family and friends. Frogs flip the kisses upside down by making something good terrible.

I can't begin to tell you about the young girls I've counseled who fell for the lies of a frog: "If you love me you will have sex with me," "No one will ever love you like I do," "I promise we will always be together," "I will take care of you if anything happens." The lies go on and on. I've sat with many good girls who allowed the kisses to go out of their boundaries because they believed that they were loved. They now sit alone, as their prince was a frog and hopped away from responsibility when things got tough. His words didn't match his actions.

The kisses of a frog's lips are flattering but they are the kisses of betrayal and if we receive them we will be brokenhearted, miserable, ashamed, and have death of sexual purity (Rom. 16:18).

God's kisses say that we are to have self-control, be patient, kind, gentle, loving, and faithful. If we receive His kisses, we will have self-confidence, self-control, joy, and peace (Galatians 5:22).

People Closest to Us

Sometimes it's the people closest to us that can hurt us the most. They are used by Satan to inflict his kisses when they lie, gossip, manipulate, defame, abuse, and abandon us (physically or emotionally).

If we receive (believe) these depraved kisses, our spirits will gradually fill up with envy, strife, jealousy, hate, bitterness, impurity, and sensuality (Galatians 5:19-20). The death of relationships and self-control is right around the corner. Most of us know this kiss well, because jealousy, lies, and gossip have been death to many good friendships.

I'll never forget the feeling I had as I walked into the high school gymnasium one Friday night. My heart was ripped out as I looked in the stands and there was my best friend holding hands with my boyfriend. How could the two of them be so dishonest, so mean? I felt humiliated. I was the last person in town to know about their crush. For two years I didn't speak to them. I hated them both.

From the time we were little, this girlfriend and I were inseparable. On the softball team we were known as Scunie and Sconnie. At the lake we water skied side by side and were known as the dynamic duo. If someone asked her to spend the night, she would ask if I could come. We were two peas in a pod. We told each other everything (at least I told her everything). She wasn't just my best friend; she was my older sister. How could she hurt me so badly? I knew I didn't want the boyfriend back but I kept thinking that she'd get tired of him and miss me, but she chose him. The hurt and bitterness took over me.

Jesus comprehends every human emotion fully. After all, He designed every detail about us and experienced them Himself as a human. He experienced the joy of great relationships. He also experienced betrayal, conflict, and sorrow similar to that which you have suffered with friends or family (Heb. 2:18).

While Jesus walked on earth, He spent a lot of time with His friends. His twelve closest friends He called disciples. But even His intimate friends disappointed Him, just like frogs, family and friends have disappointed us.

The Kiss: Friendship or Betrayal?

It was the Jewish holiday, Passover, and Jesus was breaking bread with his twelve friends, who had no idea that history was about to change. Jesus said He was going to be beaten, bruised, and suffer for them. He said He was going to die, and His blood would cover their sins. His disciples must have thought He was nuts.

After all, He healed lepers, opened deaf ears and blind eyes. He made the lame walk. He turned water into wine, raised a man from the dead, and walked on water. Surely He could defend Himself from the attackers who plotted to kill Him!

"One of you will betray Me," Jesus said.

Can you hear the disciples disagreeing with him? "No way! It's all good. None of us would ever do that!" After all, they had all given up their day jobs to follow Jesus. They had put everything on the line for Him: Family, friends, and incomes. What was left to give? Their hearts.

Jesus left the dinner party after telling His disciples He would be betrayed and walked into the garden of Gethsemane to pray. He asked three of His best friends, Peter, James and John, to be on the lookout while He prayed. His friends let Him down. They fell asleep. While Jesus confronted his three friends, a mob led by Jesus' disciple and friend Judas stormed into the garden. Judas stepped right up to Jesus and gave him a kiss (Matthew 26:48).

"Judas" Jesus said, "Are you betraying the Son of Man with a kiss?" (Luke 22:48).

Judas used the kiss of friendship *phileo* to identify Jesus to the angry mob. He turned *phileo* upside down and handed Jesus over to the enemy. That kiss cost Jesus his life.

They tortured Him, spit on Him, rolled dice for His clothes, and then hung Him on a cross, to die.

His three closest friends failed to protect Him. Judas sold Him out for thirty pieces of silver. I can't even fathom His hurt, His despair.

Nothing compares to what Jesus suffered on that cross. When Jesus asked Judas, "are you betraying the Son of Man with a kiss?" He meant, "Are you handing me over to the enemy?" The word betray means "to give over" or "deliver to the enemy." Jesus didn't try to defend Himself. He went directly to His Father (God) and said, "forgive them they know not what they do" (Luke 23:34).

Forgiving My Sister

It's been said that time heals wounds, but that's not true if you have a bitter heart. One day while vacuuming, I started thinking about how much I missed my sister. It wasn't long before anger controlled my body. In my frustration I cried out to God, "Lord, you need to do something, preferably dreadful, to her. She really hurt me!" The more I cried out to God, the madder I got. Before I knew it, I was ramming the vacuum into my walls. God in His mercy spoke gently to my heart. "June, did your sister spit on you?"

"No, Lord," I replied.

"Did she beat you beyond recognition?"

"No, Lord."

"June, did Sconnie hang you on a cross?"

"No, Lord." Tears rolled down my cheeks.

"Then, do as my Son did, and forgive her."

While on the cross, Jesus gave us a clue how to flip the kiss of betrayal back over and live "happily ever after." That clue was in forgiveness. He said, "Father, forgive them; for they do not know what they are doing" (Luke 23:34).

Jesus knows that an unforgiving heart makes us bitter, angry, resentful and gives Satan a foothold into our lives. We say and do things that we wouldn't normally do when the darts of bitterness pierce our minds and souls. When we refuse to forgive, God sees it as open rebellion toward Him. We have gone to work for the enemy. "Rebellion is as the sin of witchcraft" (I Sam. 15:23). The Hebrew word for rebellion is *meriy*, pronounced "*mer-ee.*" It means bitterness. If we allow ourselves to feel bitter, we have betrayed Jesus with a kiss of betrayal and accepted a curse from Satan.

If Jesus can forgive His friends and enemies, then we can and must forgive ours. All of us will either give or receive the kiss of betrayal sometime in our life. Turn the kiss back around, come out of Satan's workforce, and forgive.

Our tendency when kissed with betrayal is to repay that wrong with evil. God tells us, "never take your own revenge, beloved, but leave room for the wrath of God, for it is written 'Vengeance is Mine, I will repay,' says the Lord" (Rom. 12:19). Stepping on frogs, friends, or sisters and squishing them is not our job. Neither is capturing them mentally and holding them captive. Our job is to forgive them and give it to God. God gets even in ways we can't imagine! But more than getting even with them, He wants to change our bitter hearts into loving hearts because it's best for us. The day I was able to forgive my sister, a heavy ball and chain was removed from my mind. I was free to live and grateful that God didn't answer my vindictive prayers. Amen!

We have all been hurt in some way by the kiss of betrayal. Know that your hurt has not gone unnoticed. Have hope that it might just bring forth your greatest victory. Just hang on and look to Jesus. Suffering on the cross looked like His biggest defeat. Everyone who saw Him there on the cross thought the enemy had won. Satan probably ran victory laps around his captives and gave his co-fallen angels high fives. What Satan didn't realize is that Jesus was paying him a personal visit. Scripture tells us that Jesus "descended into the lower parts of the earth" (Ephesians 4:9, Psalm 16:10). "He was delivered for our sins, put on the cross, and was raised again for our justification" (Romans 4:25).

Grab hold of this!

While dying on the cross, Jesus captured every one of our sins upon Himself. It was our sins (betrayal) that killed Him. And then the Bible tells us that He covered our sins (Romans 4:7). "Covered" in the Greek means "to hide, to conceal." Jesus took care of our sins! Envision this: Jesus scooped up every sin that was ever committed and every sin that would be committed, heaved them upon His adversary Satan, and said, *"In your face!" I have conquered sin and death, now give me the keys of hell!"* (Rev. 1:18). (Italics mine). Whose high fiving now?

Then three days later, those who had believed in Him, He freed from the enemy and ascended from hell with a host of captives (Ephesians 4:8-10, Luke 16:20-26, Luke 4:18). Tombs opened and many bodies of the saints who had died rose up. Dumbfounded, they staggered out of the tombs, then entered the holy city and appeared to many (Matthew 27:52-53). That, my friend, is turning your greatest defeat into your greatest victory.

Our sins are buried, but Satan wants to project them back on us by using his kisses of betrayal. If we receive them, we sin (Genesis 4:7). We can take our sins back to the foot of the cross; ask for forgiveness, and the Prince of Peace "removes them as far as the east is from the west" (Psalm 103:12). Hallelujah! Now that's that kind of Prince I'm talking about—one who will love me, save me, and forgive me no matter what I've done; A Prince who has given His life so that I might live! Have you ever received His kisses and accepted Him as your Prince?

There are two Princes, Jesus and Satan. Fighting for your devotion and soul. One wants to give you the kiss of love, desire, deliverance; one wants to provide for you, protect you, and give you pleasure. The other offers the kiss of hurt, betrayal, and death. Don't be fooled by Satan's kisses, as they may be pleasurable for a season, but deadly in the end. Choosing the right kiss seems obvious, but at times is almost impossible to recognize because Satan is the ultimate deceiver (Rev. 12:9).

How will you know? By knowing the kisses (Truth) of Jesus—*phileo* (friendship), *chashaq* (love), and *nasaq* (passion)—so well that anything upside down is obviously betrayal.

The Shulammite girl, in her heart and soul, dreams of a better life. She has set her sights high as she dreams of kissing the king with the kisses that will change her life.

As you look for your prince, ask yourself, "Does he offer the kisses of friendship, love, and passion, within in their appropriate boundaries, or the kiss of lies, secrecy, irresponsibility, and ultimately betrayal?"

Kingdom Challenge:

Put this book down for a day! As you encounter people that you know in the next twenty-four hours, I want you to greet them with a kiss of *phileo* (greeting, friendship). Now this kiss is to be given on both cheeks, with a smack for sound. I'm not talking about some half-hearted kiss. I'm talking about a relational kiss. Now after you've kissed this person, you cannot talk bad about them or even have bad thoughts about them. In fact, if you don't come to their defense when someone else is trashing them, your kiss of friendship has just turned into the kiss of betrayal. Your friends are going to ask you about the kiss. Share with them what you're learning in *Wake Up Sleeping Beauty*.

Today's One-Liner: ....Jesus is Prince of Peace
Clue for living "Happily Ever After" .... Ephesians 6: 11-12

> *Put on the full armor of God, that you may be able to stand firm against the schemes of the devil. For our struggle is not against flesh and blood, but against the rulers, against the powers, against the world forces of this darkness, against the spiritual forces of wickedness in the heavenly places*

Kiss of Love:...Forgiveness
Kiss of Betrayal:.. Bitterness

Chapter Two

What's In A Name?

"Your oils have a pleasing fragrance,
Your name is like purified oil;
Therefore the maidens love you."
Song of Solomon 1:3

Have you ever admired someone from afar; maybe the quarterback of the football team, or the boy setting next to you in science class, or possibly someone famous? You know their name, you know a lot of facts about them, but you don't know them personally, and they have no idea who you are.

Solomon's name intrigues the Shulammite girl. She can't get him out of her mind. As he passes her in the vineyard she gives him a flirtatious look and her heart skips a beat. She's dreaming about spending time with him; perhaps, dinner and a movie? Wonder what's playing at the Jerusalem Carmike? "Gladiator"? Bumping into him in the vineyard on occasion isn't enough; she longs to know him personally.

We can all identify with the Shulammite girl as she enters into the beginning stages of wanting a relationship. She begins inquiring and pursuing her far-fetched dream of dating the king.

A few years ago, I laughed as I watched my daughter and her friends have this Shulammite mentality. They all drooled over Orlando Bloom. He played Legolas, the hunk in "Lord of the Rings." They didn't know him personally, but they read about him in magazines and watched him in the movies. My daughter, Jerrilyn, would have loved to have known him personally. I knew how she felt about him by the life-sized, cardboard poster that stood next to her bed. Many times I walked by Jerri's room and jumped with fright, thinking that there was a strange man in our house, only to realize that it was just a six-foot, look-alike of Orlando. Orlando's cardboard statue jokingly filled in for prom dates that didn't make it to our home in time for pictures.

Dressed in her beautiful wedding gown, Jerrilyn took one last picture with Orlando. She had to let him down gently. We all laughed, as her fantasy of marrying the perfect prince was about to come true. However, it was not society's dream man that she married; it was God's warrior.

Our Shulammite girl knows that just because Solomon has the title of king behind his name doesn't mean that he's a true prince. She will research Solomon's name, to save herself future headaches and heartaches. But after going undercover, asking lots of questions, doing her homework, and relying on insight of friends and family she returns to us with a report, "Your oils have a pleasing fragrance; your name is like purified oil; therefore the maidens love you" (Song of Solomon 1:3).

According to her findings, a true prince must have three credentials: (1) Great cologne; (2) A great name; (3) Be related to the "Prince of Peace."

He Has Great Cologne

Comparing Solomon's name to perfume means he's sweet to be around. God is telling us to find someone who is easy to be with. Someone you really enjoy. He doesn't stink; you can see this because of the company he keeps. When you are checking out a guy, look at who he hangs out with and watch what kind of people he attracts. Let's look at some ways to detect good-smelling cologne.

Tip # 1: Check Him Out

Before our daughters can ever go out on a date with a guy, we check around with people that know him. We are doing a "background check" on his character and finding out who he hangs out with and what type of person he is. We ask friends questions like "How well do you know this person? Would you let your daughter date him? What's his family like?" and so forth. I remember one fellow who didn't check out too well; so we wouldn't let our daughter, Jolene, date him. She was convinced that our sources were wrong and begged us to reconsider. We didn't give in. About five years later, Jolene was reading the local paper and saw that a warrant was out for his arrest. Her reaction was priceless: "I'll be darned," she said. "Look who made the local blotter?" The blotter is where they post any DUI, theft, or criminal activity in the local newspaper. "Yeah, you could have been the next 'Bonnie' as in 'Bonnie and Clyde,'" we teased. After all the joking, she said she really appreciated the fact that we cared enough to find out about him, and to say "no."

We were pretty careful about checking out the girls' boyfriends, but we were amateurs compared to a friend of mine who worked for the Dallas Police Department. He was so concerned about a guy his sixteen-year-old daughter was dating that he ran a criminal check on him. Sure enough, the boy had a record. The daughter didn't care. She liked this bad boy; he was intriguing to her. The father was relentless as he did everything he could to try to protect his daughter from making a huge mistake. He tapped her phone, checked on her whereabouts. He did everything but tie her to the bedpost.

My friend told me that the greatest day of his life was when his daughter finally realized that her daddy wasn't trying to make her life miserable; he was trying to keep her from being miserable.

It's imperative that we listen to the counsel of our parents and not go sneaking around with some guy that they don't approve of. "Children, obey your parents in the Lord, for this is right. Honor you father and mother (which is the first commandment with a promise), so that it may be well with you and that you may live long on the earth" (Ephesians 6:1-3). Ask your parents to help you research your potential date; they have smelled many colognes and know a good one when they smell it.

If we were to check out the Prince of Peace, Jesus, we would find that He attracted all kinds of people: the wealthy, the sick, the prostitutes, and the cheating tax collectors. At first glance, we might think that He was wearing bad cologne, but if we investigate further we will see that Jesus' sweet-smelling fragrance is what drew them in and eventually changed their lives. The difference is, he was perfect and was able to change and heal them, not be negatively influenced by them.

What kinds of people are attracted to your prince's cologne? Does he change when he's around them for the worse or are people changed for the better from his presence?

He Has a Great Name:

"Name" in Hebrew means "character," which means "to engrave, to mark something, to show ownership." Character is the attributes or features that make up and distinguish the individual. The Shulammite is saying that Solomon has great character. Solomon's name has depth. He is more than just a pretty face.

A man's character is engraved into him much like initials are engraved into a tree trunk. As that tree grows, the initials grow with it. They get bigger and bigger. This is how it is with character. If you're mean-spirited, you become meaner. If you're honest with little, you will be honest with much.

Solomon's character came out as he ruled his people. He was fair, wise, and showed no favoritism (1 Kings 3:16). His character came out as he built the temple for God. He was an efficient hard worker and did what he said he would do (1 Kings 9:1). So how does one research character?

Tip # 2: Observe His Character

One sure way to test a boy's character is to observe how he treats his own mother. Observe his behavior when he doesn't know you're watching.

For years, I've told my girls, "If he can't be nice to his mother, he won't have a clue how to be nice to you." "A wise son makes a father glad, but a foolish man despises his mother" (Proverbs 15:20).

Tip # 3: Experience His Character

I suggest you play Monopoly with him. You might be laughing, but I'm telling you that you can find out a lot about a person's character by playing games with him. You can see if he's a pouter or cheater. Is he a good sport when he loses? Is he a gracious winner? How aggressive is he? Does he take risks? Is he a good money manager? These are just a few things you can observe, while—at the same time—deciding whether or not you are enjoying his company.

One of our daughter's boyfriends lost every time he played Monopoly with my husband, Jay. Instead of quitting, he purchased the game for himself and played his family members until he was confident he could beat Jay. He came back strong as he worked a few other family members over, but he couldn't beat my man! I gave this young man an "A" for effort and perseverance. I loved this guy (maybe that's why our daughter stopped dating him!). It is imperative to know a young man's character, so find as many ways as you can to bring out his true character (name).

"He who is slow to anger is better than the mighty, and he who rules his spirit, than he who captures a city" (Proverbs 16:32).

What about the Name of Jesus?

Jesus' name is so important that prophets foretold it: "Behold the virgin shall be with child and shall bear a Son, and they shall call His name Immanuel, which translated means, 'God with us'" (Matthew 1:23). It was so important that an angel was sent from God to tell His parents what to name him. They called him *Messiah Yeshua* in Hebrew and in Greek, Jesus Christ. *Yeshua* (Jesus) means: "The Lord is Salvation." Messiah (Christ) means: "anointed one." Jesus' name means "anointed" or "set apart" to be our Savior. God has a special purpose for Jesus' life. His job: To save us from the curses of sin and deliver us from Satan's dungeon.

His name is holy and incredible but the power and character of His name is almost indescribable. Scripture tells us that His name is so powerful that those who believe in His name can ask Him anything in His name and He will do it (John 14:14). Those who believe and call on His name can cast out demons in His name and they will flee (Mark 16:17). On the basis of faith in His name, it is the name of Jesus, which gives perfect health (Acts 3:16). But the greatest power in the name of Jesus, is anyone who calls upon it will be saved (Acts 2:21).

"God highly exalted Him, and bestowed on Him the name which is above every name" (Philippians 2:9). What name gives you troubles? Is it loneliness? Loneliness is a name. Jesus' name is greater (higher) than loneliness. Is it insecurity, finances, relationships, fear, torment, sickness, jealousy? Jesus' name is greater than them all. The great Prince of Peace has the power to rescue you from them all. Believe and call on His name.

I love the name of Jesus so much that my daughter Jacque said to me one day, "Mom, you are like a high school girl who is always talking about her new boyfriend." Have you heard about my new, old, and forever boyfriend, Jesus? His name means "God is with us" and He is "set apart to be our savior" not just our eternal savior but also our physical savior right here, right now (Is.53: 4-5). He is such a character. He's flawless, loving, healing, saving, delivering and freeing.

Have you admired Him from afar? Perhaps it's time to get to know Him personally.

How is your earthly prince doing so far? Is he passing the test? Is he fun to be around? Are his friends losers or fun to hang with? How does he treat his mother? How's his character holding up? Do you want to keep pursuing him or is it time to let him down gently? If your man wears great cologne and has great character (name) then it's time to see if he passes challenge tip number four and survives the family.

Tip # 4: Take an Island Vote

Every boyfriend or girlfriend has had to meet at least part of our large family. After meeting them and spending some time with them, a family vote is taken to decide whether or not the boyfriend or girlfriend gets to stay on the island.

This year we've had four new recruits. All of them have been warned about the island procedure. My niece's boyfriend, Nick was a shoo-in as he was a youth minister and called me Miss June. I was sure to influence the tribal vote.

You could see the love for Hillary through Nick's eyes. He opened doors for her and spoke kindly to her and about her even when she wasn't around. He was always asking Hillary, "What do you think about such and such?" The respect he had for her and her family showed as he kept her pure until marriage.

My nephew's girlfriend was from Kentucky and we all loved her. She was full of life and loved the outdoors, which goes a long way in a family full of sports fanatics. She also received a few votes when we found out she had access to box seats at the Kentucky Derby. Just kidding! However, there was one major problem, she wasn't in love with my nephew. It was obvious as she often picked her friends and her own ambitions before him. Selfishness has no place in a marriage relationship.

Our daughter's boyfriend was embraced as we all appreciated the fact that he loved her and was on his way to Iraq to fight for us. Who could throw him off the island? His character was full of integrity.

As for the fourth candidate, the vote is not yet in.

Not everyone who shows up on the "family island" makes it. Some are thrown off by the "dater" after they've been accepted. Some decide they'd rather swim to the next island than to have anything to do with this crazy family (I can't really blame them)! Yet there is one criterion that has stood firm for generations in the tribe: He or she must be related to and love the Prince of Peace.

Is He Related to the "Prince of Peace?"

". . . Your name is like purified oil . . ." (Song of Solomon 1:3).

Purified oil to the Hebrews was sacred. It meant bright, pure, uncontaminated, innocent, and holy. The priest used it to consecrate or set apart kings, priests and or holy objects for God's special purpose. The Shulammite girl is complimenting Solomon on his pure, Godly name, as it means "beloved by God."

Having your name compared to purified (anointing) oil was the highest compliment one could give. It would be horrifying to Solomon if his name were compared to our modern-day, motor oil.

In the day of Solomon, your name preceded you. People knew all about you because of your family and they knew who you were related to. You can probably identify with this if you have older brothers or sisters in school. You probably receive favor if your older siblings were well liked by teachers. On the flip side, you might always have to prove yourself if your sibling were troublemakers.

A name is valuable, and we should all work hard to keep our family's name and others' pure. The way we live and talk affects not only us, but also others. We need to remember the next time we are in the mist of talking about somebody that we could be turning their purified name into motor oil. When we start to talk about somebody, let's ask ourselves, "would we be saying these things if this person were standing next to us?" If the answer is "no," we need to stop talking.

So how about the guy you admire? Does his family's name represent motor oil or purified oil?

Tip # 5: Check out His Family!

As we observe his family we need to ask ourselves: Are they respected? Do they respect others? Who are they related to? If and when I have children, would I want them to spend a lot of time with these people? Do I enjoy these people? What do they do for fun? Are they related to the Prince of Peace? Are they Godly?

The reason I'm making such a big deal about families, their names and character is that many of you have the desire to marry someday. On your wedding day you will be making a covenant with someone, and your name will change. His name will become your name; his family will become your family.

It's so important that you check out the family's history so that you can see patterns and understand the family's character, because whether you like it or not, his family will become yours.

I imagine our Shulammite girl came to the conclusion that Solomon's name was "purified" after she researched his family. She was probably fascinated as she stumbled onto a great-great-great grandfather (fifteen times removed) named Abram, and I'm sure she was impressed to know that Solomon's family was in a covenant with the Almighty God.

A covenant is a spiritual agreement between two people. It is a lifetime commitment—until death do you part.

I heard a preacher, Creflo A. Dollar, describe covenant something like this:

> Let's say on one side of town you have the Farmers and on the other side of town you have the Warriors. The Warriors keep killing the Farmers and taking their food. The Warriors soon realize that if they keep killing the Farmers, they are going to starve to death because they don't know how to grow corn, wheat, or rye. So the Warrior Chief goes to the head Farmer and says, "I really think we need each other. Let's make an agreement. We, the Warriors, will protect you, the Farmers, if you will grow food for us. You will never have to worry about enemies because we will protect you. In return we will never have to worry about food because you will feed us.
>
> Now at this point, the head Farmer can either accept the agreement or reject it, but he cannot change it (Galatians 3:15). The head Farmer, accepts and they get all of their people together for the big ceremony. The Farmers are on one side of the field and the Warriors on the other. The Chief Warrior and Head Farmer kill a bull in front of the people and then they hang it up. They then cut the bull in half so that the bull's blood is pouring on the ground. The blood from each side of the bull has now dipped into one pool of blood. You can no longer tell which half the blood came from. The Chief and the Head Farmer walk through the two halves and get the blood on their feet, representing that the Farmers and the Warriors are one team. This is a blood covenant. The Chief and his people and the Farmer and his people then cut the palms of their hands, so that they scar. The scar is a sign of the covenant. Anyone who saw the Farmer's scar knew that he was in covenant with someone. They knew not to mess with the Farmer, especially when they saw the

> matching scar on the Warrior's hand. The only way this covenant could be broken was by death. Does this ceremony remind you of anything; perhaps a wedding?

Solomon's great-great-great grandfather (fifteen times removed) receives a call from God. God said, "Abram, I want you to leave your home. I want you to take your wife and your servants and go to a land that I'm going to give you. I'm going to make you a great nation, and I will bless you, (through wealth, descendants, and land) and make your name great; and so you shall be a blessing. In fact I will bless those who bless you, and the one who curses you I will curse" (Genesis 12: 1-3). So Abram loaded up his wife, Sarai, and Lot, his nephew, and all their possessions, along with their hired help, and pursued God.

Ten years later, Abram was very wealthy and had acquired the promise land, but there was no heir. Was the promised son . . . "in you all the families of the earth will be blessed" (Genesis 12:3) . . . just a figment of Abram's imagination? Could he really count on God's Word? After waiting and wondering, the Word of the Lord came to Abram in a vision. "Do not fear, Abram, I am a shield to you; Your reward shall be very great" (Genesis 15).

Abram was old and said, "What can you give me since I'm wealthy and old and I have no descendants to pass it on to?" (Genesis 15:2). Up until this point I think Abram was a lot like us. He probably thought that God had given him all of his wealth because he had worked so hard, and well, the promise land was just a smart investment that God had suggested. But there was no way that he was going to have a son at the age of 85. It just wasn't physically possible! And so far every word that he had obtained was physically possible in his own human strength. So I imagine Abram's attitude to be "don't even bother, God, this isn't possible. I'm too old." This is exactly where God wanted Abram, unable to perform, relying on God for a miracle.

"Look at the stars in the sky. Can you count them?" God said. "Just as you can't count all the stars, you won't be able to count all of your descendants either because there will be so many" (Genesis 15:5). Can you imagine the change of heart that Abram had as the God of the universe began to speak to him and show him His great creation? I can't imagine how small Abram must have felt as God assured him that having a son at the age of 85 was nothing for God to make happen.

Abram's faith took a huge leap as he replied with an "Amen" which means "to confirm or I believe." He didn't know how it would happen, he just believed it would: "Then he believed in the LORD; and God reckoned it to him as righteousness" (Genesis 15:6). Abram was saved and in an eternal covenant with God, because from this moment on Abram believed that through him would come "the seed" (Jesus Christ) in whom all the families of the earth would be blessed (Galatians 3:16). In other words every family would have the chance to have this covenant through faith in Jesus Christ.

I tell you this because so many people think that the people of the Old Testament were saved by keeping the Law of Moses, and many people today think that good works saves them. Just like Abram, believing in God's Word, believing on His Son's name alone, saves us.

God saw that Abram was righteous and therefore they proceeded to the covenant ceremony. God told Abram, "Bring Me a three-year-old heifer and a three-year-old female goat and a three-year-old ram, a turtledove, and a young pigeon." Then he brought all these to Him and cut them in two and laid each half opposite the other but he did not cut the birds. God himself walked between the pieces of meat (His presence was evident by the fire and smoke). While both parties are to walk through the pieces of meat, in this case God walked through the halves by Himself, showing the obligation for the fulfillment of the promises was on Himself alone (Genesis 15:9-21). Abram didn't have to do anything but believe.

When God made this covenant with Abram He promised three things: (1) Provision: "I will make you a great nation, and I will bless you, and make your name great; and so you shall be a blessing" (Genesis 12:2). In other words, anything that Abram touched God would prosper (Deuteronomy 28:1-14). (2) Protection: "I will bless those who bless you and the one who curses you I will curse" (Genesis 2:3). (3) Pleasure: "In you all the families of the earth shall be blessed" (Genesis 12:3). Now how do you suppose they got all those families here? Yep, through lots of pleasure . . . sex! God is showing us a picture of intimacy. We get great families from great intimacy. We get a great relationship with God through intimacy, becoming one with Him.

In the days of Solomon these are the three things a man would have to promise his wife. He would have to promise her food (provision), clothing (protection), and conjugal rights (sexual pleasure). He could not take them away from her (Exodus 21:10).

Abram's Part of the Covenant:

Abram's only responsibility in this covenant with God was to believe (Genesis 15:6).

That's it! Believe in what God said He would do. Not only believe in God, but also believe in what God said He would do. That's it—believe! Have faith!

Oh, how quickly our faith gets sidetracked when someone else comes along and tells us that there is no way that God could have said that. Abram's faith is weakened when his wife Sarai thinks she knows the intent of God's heart and plan.

Sarai was past childbearing years and didn't have the faith to believe in God's great plan so she insisted that Abram take Hagar, her Egyptian servant, as his wife. "Perhaps I will obtain children through her Sarai said (Genesis 16:2). I can just hear Abram's reasoning, his justifying: Of course this makes more sense. God wants me to take a younger wife because God wants me to have an heir." While this was politically correct in that time it was not godly correct. Abram slept with Hagar and she conceived.

It's funny how when you do things your own way and not God's way, it has a way of backfiring on you. Sarai became very jealous of Hagar and treated her poorly. Hagar ran away and cried out to the Lord. The Lord had compassion for her. An angel appeared to her and said, "I will greatly multiply your descendants so that they shall be too many to count. Behold, you are with child and you shall bear a son and call him Ishmael which means God hears. He's going to become the father of twelve princes and have a great nation under him" (Genesis 16:10-11). The angel told Hagar that Ishmael would be a wild donkey of a man. His hand would be against everyone and everyone's hand would be against him. The angel also said that Ishmael would live to the east of all his brothers (Genesis 12:12).

The Lord appears to Abram again at the age of ninety-nine and says, "I am God Almighty. Walk before Me, and be blameless" (Genesis 17:1). Abram was not blameless, as he was still depending on himself, not God, for the promised son.

God in His mercy and grace starts over with Abram and Sarai. He begins by giving them new names. Abram's name which means "father of many" was changed to Abraham, which means "father of many nations." Sarai's name, which means "my princess", was changed to Sarah, which means "princess." Talk about the power of a name! Just by changing a few letters the whole dynamic of their names change.

Abraham's Sign of the Covenant

God told Abraham that there would now be a sign of this covenant; every male living among Abraham should be circumcised in the flesh of their foreskin (penis). And every male born should be circumcised on the eighth day. The word "circumcision" means, "to cut away flesh." Ouch! God was, and is; showing us through the physical what is going on in the spiritual. He wants to cut away our flesh so that we depend on Him.

God went one step further in helping Abraham. He spoke to Sarah (the unbeliever) and helped her to believe in the impossible (Genesis 18:10-14).

After Abraham's flesh was cut away through circumcision Abraham and Sarah birthed a son at the ripe old ages of 100 and 91. Abraham fell on his face and laughed when Isaac (a name that means "he laughs") was born. The long-awaited Isaac brought laughter and joy to his parents.

God chose Abraham because He knew that he would pass the covenant down to the next generation (Genesis 18:19). He told Abraham that if he would indeed obey God's voice and keep God's covenant, then he would be God's own possession among all the peoples, for all the earth is God's (Exodus 19:5). God is saying to Abraham, "I will be your God and bless you. Pass it down!"

Abraham now believed and obeyed. Faith in God's promise saved Abraham; being obedient to God's voice brought forth His blessing, Jesus Christ (Matthew 1:1-17).

The Shulammite girl would be foolish not to pursue Solomon. He wears great cologne, his name is great, and he and his family are related to the "Prince of Peace." Not to mention that if she married Solomon she would inherit the fortunes of Abraham.

"If we belong to Christ (not just know a lot of facts about Him, but know Him personally) then we are Abraham's descendants, heirs according to promise" (Galatians 3:29). We are related to the Prince of Peace when we accept Him, and believe that He is our Savior.

Does the guy that you are admiring belong to Jesus Christ? If yes, he is related to the "Prince of Peace." If no, it might be time to stop the pursuit.

Don't get me wrong. I'm not saying that we should not date a non-believer. If I did I would be a hypocrite. When I first started dating my husband he was not a believer. My high school business teacher confronted me about it. He shared with me that it's hard to raise kids, make financial decisions, and grow deep spiritually when two people don't agree religiously. He showed me in scripture where it stated that an unbeliever is not to be bound to a believer (II Corinthians 6:14-15).

I took a stand, drew a line in the sand. I was not going to marry a non-believer. If we are believers in Christ, before we become too serious, before we give the kiss of *chashaq* to someone, he needs to be a believer for us to receive the full blessings of our covenant with God.

When we marry we enter into a blood covenant. We become one. Scripture tells us "you shall not plow with an ox and a donkey together" (Deuteronomy 22:10). The step and pull of the two beasts is unequal. Imagine yourself literally tied to someone for the rest of your life who will not walk along side you with God. Eventually you will be pulled apart. Abraham and Sarah didn't receive the full covenant until they both believed. If you want to receive the full blessings of God's covenant, you and your prince must be related to the "Prince of Peace."

If only Princess Aurora had asked the stranger in the woods his name, smelled his cologne, and realized that he was the prince, she would have saved herself from the headaches and the curse of Maleficent.

Are you admiring someone from afar? Does he wear great-smelling cologne, have a great name, and is he related to the "Prince of Peace?" If he has all of these credentials, keep pursuing him. If you're not sure, let's find out.

Kingdom Challenge:

I want you to put this book down for a few days while we go undercover. We are going to do a background check on two characters: Jesus and someone who intrigues you. First, we will determine what kind of cologne they wear (what kind of people they hang with). Second, we are going to find out at about their names. We will list at least three of their character traits. Is he good to his mom? Is he honest? Is he hot-tempered, truthful, and so forth? Is his name purified oil or motor oil? Is he related to the "Prince of Peace?" When you are done with the investigation, enjoy reading chapter three.

Character #1: The Guy Who Intrigues You

(1) Cologne: ____________________

(2) Name (character traits): ____________________

(3) Purified oil or motor oil? ____________________

(4) Related to: ____________________

Character #2: Jesus

(1) Cologne: ____

(2) Name (character traits): ______________________________

(3) Purified oil or motor oil? ______________________________

(4) Related to: ____

Today's One-Liner: .... Jesus, Set apart to be our Savior
Clue for living "Happily Ever After" .... Proverbs 22:1

"A good name is to be more desired than great wealth."

Kiss of Love: .... Belief in God's Word
Kiss of Betrayal: .... Unbelief

Chapter Three

A Ridiculous Request

"Draw me after you and let us run together!"
Song of Solomon 1:4

Before we begin this chapter I want to ask you two questions: What is your heart's greatest desire? You know that really big dream that is deep within your soul. And what is your greatest fear?

Being from a country that gives equal rights to women, it would be hard for us to imagine how scary it might be for a young girl who has no rights, no security, and no guarantee of protection or provision until she is married.

Our Shulammite girl is fully aware of her predicament and therefore after investigating Solomon she boldly states: "Draw me to you and let us run together" (Song of Solomon 1:4). What a ridiculous request; a peasant girl pleading to run with the king! She's not only desiring to run with him, she's asking to be drawn to him. The Hebrew word for "draw" is *meshek*, which means "a sowing, a possession, precious, price." Her desire is for Solomon to cherish, honor, and possess her, she dreams of becoming his wife. Marrying Solomon will change her life forever and marrying will change your life forever!

In our last chapter we talked about what kind of criteria we wanted our prince to have. He is to have a great name, wear great-smelling cologne, and be related to the "Prince of Peace." Why would a prince like that want us? Why would Solomon be the least bit interested in the Shulammite girl? What criteria are the princes of old and the princes of today looking for?

Out of curiosity, I looked on the Internet to see what today's men wanted in a woman. I looked at secular as well as Christian web sites. Here's what they had to say:

Christian boys between 13-18:

"A girl who is happy with herself, you know someone who's not worried about her hair and clothes all the time."
"A girl who stands up for what she thinks and is outgoing."
"She takes care of herself."
"A Christian"
"A sense of humor and is interested in sports."
"Good moral values."
"She's not too easy to catch!"
"Physically attractive"

Secular boys between 13-18:

"Have ability to tease."
"Calls us out of the blue."
"Enjoy a good debate."
"Enjoy sports."
"Is charming and thoughtful to his mother"
"Spirit of independence but doesn't make the man feel unnecessary."
"Know the difference between flirting and being friendly."
"Knows what she wants."
"Knows what she wants to do."
"Physically attractive"
"Looks, if you want a fling—Character, if you want a wife."

I found it interesting that both secular and Christian males are looking for the same three things in a woman: (1) Faith (Christian boys want a woman with faith in God; secular boys wants a woman with faith in herself.); (2) Physical beauty (takes care of herself, neatly dressed, and well groomed, clean, good posture); and (3) Character (moral values, purity).

Kings, whether Godly or secular, also had three criteria when looking for a wife; she had to be: (1) young; (2) beautiful; (3) and a virgin (Esther 2:2).

When King David needed someone to take care of him, they sought after a young, beautiful virgin (I King 1:2-3). When King Ahasuerus, who was a secular king, was looking for a bride, all the young, beautiful virgins were brought to the palace (Esther 2:2). When Abraham's servant was looking for a bride for Isaac, he found a very beautiful virgin named Rebekah (Genesis 24:16). When God picked Mary she was a young virgin who was undoubtedly beautiful. God has the same standards when picking a bride for His Son. He will make no exceptions; she is to be young, beautiful, and a virgin.

We have been led astray thinking that guys only want one thing: sex! That's not true; he desires his wife to be a young, beautiful virgin.

Before you throw up your hands and give up because you don't feel you meet these standards you need to know that God can and will make all things new (II Cor. 5:17). This chapter is all about you. It's all about you becoming a young, beautiful virgin.

The Protocol of the Kingdom

In order for us to understand the depth of the Shulammite girl's ridiculous request, we must understand the protocol of the kingdom. God gave us a clear picture of the rules and regulations of the Heavenly Kingdom when He instructed Moses how to build and operate in an earthly structure called the Tabernacle (Solomon's temple was built in the same fashion). This structure was divided into three sections: an upper or inner court, the Holy Place, and the Holy of Holies (where God rules and reigns on His throne). If we can learn how to get through the sections of the tabernacle and to the heart of God, we will learn how to get through the palace and to the heart of a King.

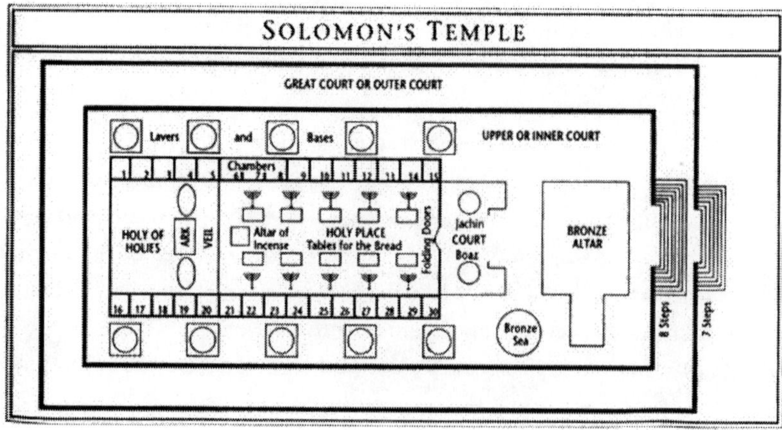

Kingdom Rule # 1: (You have to be called)

No one is allowed near the king unless he draws you or summons you to himself. If you try to enter into the inner chamber where the king reigns on his throne when you aren't called, there is one consequence—death—unless the king extends mercy to you by holding out his golden scepter. Only then your life may be spared (Esther 4:11).

Fear has been a tactic used to keep people away from kings from the beginning of kingdoms, and Satan will use fear as a kiss of betrayal to keep you away from the King's—God's—throne as well. Satan doesn't want you to get near the King where you might ask your ridiculous requests and live in the moments of grandeur that God has planned for you.

Fear will keep us from doing God's will. It keeps us in our mediocre life and away from the amazing destiny that the Lord has called us to. It will keep us out of the King's throne room and toiling in the vineyard.

Faith, on the other hand, moves the heart of God. God tells us, "Without faith it is impossible to please Him, for he who comes to God must believe that He is and that He is a rewarder of those who seek Him" (Hebrew 11:6).

If you had the faith to stand before God, what ridiculous requests would you make? What dreams, what visions do you have for your life? Think big! Dream! Imagine huge! Know that God is capable and wants to do more than you've ever asked or imagined!

I have many ridiculous requests but I want to share one with you: I pray that *Wake Up, Sleeping Beauty* is published. I want girls to learn how to walk in covenant with the Lord. I desire girls to know the protocol of the Kingdom so that they might go from an acquaintance of God to knowing Him intimately. My dream is that they don't just enter into the kingdom gates but that they venture into His inner chamber and receive His favor and His blessings on their lives. If you're reading this, then you know that this prayer has been answered.

God wants us to come to Him with our ridiculous requests. So how do we get His attention? Where is He ruling and reigning and how do we get into His chamber without getting our heads chopped off? Our first clue comes from the Shulammite girl. She is asking to be drawn to Solomon. What she doesn't know is that Solomon is way ahead of her. He has already been drawing her to himself. The vineyard she works in isn't just any vineyard; it belongs to Solomon (Song of Solomon 8:10-11). He has been watching her from afar. He has been flirting with her, passing by to give her a glance of his kindness, wooing her with his name and character. She has no idea that he has been captivating her heart all along.

Jesus tells us, "No one can come to Him unless the Father who sent Him draws him" (John 6:44). The word "draws" is the same word the Shulammite girl used. However in the Greek it is helko (hell-ko), which literally means, "to drag."

God draws us to the Prince of Peace, to His palace, two different ways: One, He uses the Holy Spirit to gently woo us—as Solomon did the Shulammite girl—through his love, his character, his sweet-smelling fragrance. Two, He uses His Holy Spirit to drag us in kicking and screaming.

Whether it is by wooing or dragging, one thing is for sure, God is drawing you to His Son, Jesus. I know this because you're reading this book. He's been flirting with you and you are interested to know more about Him.

Do you know that without Him you have no rights, no security, no protection or provision? Do you know that He is the man who will change your life forever?

So now that we've been drawn to the palace we need to know how to get into the inner courts.

Kingdom Rule # 2: Entering the Courts—Young Faith

The people of Israel knew that they didn't deserve to be in the courts of God because they had sinned against Him. They had broken their covenant with Him and deserved death. But God in His mercy and grace allowed sacrifices to take their sins' place.

Many people brought their sacrifices daily to the inner court of the temple: a bull, a goat, a dove, depending upon the sin and their financial status. They would place their hands upon the animal as it was being sacrificed, which represented that all of their sins were transferred to the animal. This animal took their sins and was the one to die, instead of that person. This cleansed the person who offered the sacrifice and made them acceptable before God. These sacrifices took place on the bronze altar that was in the inner court.

We enter through the palace gates and into the inner court when we place our faith in Jesus Christ. He took our sins and was the one to die as we sacrificed Him on the cross at Calvary. Picture yourself laying your hands on Jesus as He died on the cross; all of your sins were transferred to Him. "It is by grace you have been saved, through faith—and this not from yourselves, it is the gift of God—not by works, so that no one can boast" (Ephesians 2:8-9).

Once you enter His courts you meet the "Prince's" first criteria: faith. Kings, however, want that and more. They want youth too!

For years women have been trying to find the "fountain of youth." Magazines tell us it comes in a bottle of makeup or perfume. Health clubs claim that it comes from exercise. Doctors boost their claims by selling us pills. Jesus tells us something different. He says that He is the living water and unless you are converted and "become like children, you will not enter the kingdom of heaven" (Matthew 18:2). The secret to youth is to depend on Jesus like children depend on their parents.

Our faith in Christ alone gets us into His courts; our dependence upon Him keeps us young, because we won't be worrying about the things that cause wrinkles.

My grandmother Grace died at the age of 96. When she died she hardly had any wrinkles. Most people called her "Amazing Grace" and attributed her youthful looks to the Vaseline that she rubbed on her face every night. I know differently. There wasn't a day that went by that my grandmother didn't read and study her Bible. Her faith in Christ and His promises kept her young and wrinkle-free.

If you have entered into His courts then you know what Solomon's dad meant when he said, "Better is one day in His courts than a thousand elsewhere" (Psalm 84:10).

If you haven't entered His courts, simply believe and ask Jesus to forgive you for your sins and ask Him to be your savior. "If you confess with your mouth, "Jesus is Lord," and believe in your heart that God raised him from the dead, you will be saved. For it is with your heart that you believe and are justified, and it is with your mouth that you confess and are saved" (Rom.10: 9-10). Put your hand out and know that all of your sins have been transferred onto Him. You have been cleansed and are acceptable before Christ.

Many will come into God's inner court and receive the benefit of eternal life, but they will never truly experience kingdom life, because God requires more than just faith to enter into His Holy Place and run with Him.

Kingdom Rule # 3: Entering the Holy Place—Beauty

Only the Levi Priests were allowed to enter into the Holy Place. God chose the Levites because they were the only tribe out of the twelve that sided with God instead of with the people (Exodus 32:26).

Distraught after learning God's teaching on purity, one young girl came to me with an attitude: "I'm having sex, and I'm not stopping. No one has the right to tell me how to live my life," she said, crossing her arms and glaring at me.

The glare softened to sadness as she spoke again. "My whole family is cursed."

"What do you mean?" I asked.

Tears shimmered in her eyes. "There's not one person in the whole family that's ever stayed married. It's like nobody has any loyalty!"

I thought for a moment, and then said, "Do you still think your ways, the world's standards, are better than God's?"

I truly believe this girl is a believer in Jesus Christ, but unless she changes her thinking and behavior, she will miss out on the amazing life that God has in store for her. Sadly, there are many Christians who will spend their whole life right outside the palace door. They will always date God but will never be engaged or married to Him. They will never enjoy the perks of living inside the palace walls: the banquets, spa treatments, fine clothing, and preferential treatment.

After one becomes a princess (a Christian), it is up to the individual whether or not she wants to walk in the ways of the kingdom. Yet, to get into the Holy Place it's a requirement.

In the movie "The Princess Diaries," the unpopular, awkward, suburban teenager finds out that she is not a peasant, but is of royal blood (like Sleeping Beauty).

Being an heir to the throne didn't mean that all of a sudden she knew the ways of the kingdom. The queen (who happened to be her grandmother), showed her how a princess should act. At first she really fought it. She didn't like the edict of the kingdom. She didn't want someone telling her how to act. She didn't like being different than her friends. However, there were huge perks in the palace life: chauffeurs, butlers, financial security, and VIPs.

It was hard work, and at times, it took her away from the things and people that she loved. But if she was ever going to learn how to rule and reign as the queen, it was essential that she show up for her daily lessons.

At the end of the movie, the princess not only became poised, she was transformed into a knockout, eye-catching, breathtaking, beautiful young woman.

This is exactly how it is in the Holy Place. First we must choose whether or not we want to walk the ways of God. God's ways won't come to us all at once; and they won't always be easy. We will need the Holy Spirit to teach us. We will feel awkward, out of place, and at times alone. Friends may not choose to go with us and life won't be as it once was. But in the end, if we are obedient to His ways, we will enjoy the incredible perks of the Kingdom and we will come out transformed, jaw dropping, traffic stopping, drop-dead gorgeous!

The scripture tell us that God has placed us a little lower than God and has crowned us with glory and honor (Psalms 8:4-5). In temple terms, I believe this crown is for those in the Holy Place as it is right below the Holy of Holies (where God dwells). Common people in the outer courts don't wear crowns. The crown is a huge benefit for those who choose God's ways, as the Hebrew word for "glory" means "splendor," while "honor" in the Hebrew language means "beauty, Excellency, majesty, and to favor." God is telling us that when we enter the Holy Place we aren't who we think we are. We are not common people. We are princesses! (Sound like Sleeping Beauty?) He has a crown for us. He desires for us to learn His ways so that He might pour His glory (splendor) and honor on us. We will have special advantages, see amazing things, soak in His precious anointing oils; wear the finest jewels and beautiful clothing. People will start giving us preferential treatment. Do you dare to enter into this spiritual Kingdom that pours out natural blessings?

If you answered "yes" to my question, then raise your hands up. It doesn't matter if you're in a plane, car, at school, or reading this in bed, raise your hands high and say to God, "Show me your ways!"

Before the priest entered into the Holy Place, Moses said: "This is what the LORD has commanded you to do, so that the glory of the LORD may appear to you" (Leviticus 9:6 NIV).

Oh, to see His glory! The Israelites had been privileged to witness it many times. They experienced His glory when He parted the seas and brought water out of a rock and heard His voice in the clouds. They testified to His glory earlier when He rained down bread from heaven (Exodus 16:4-6).

Forget catching snowflakes in your mouth. How about going out and catching Great Harvest cinnamon bread every morning for breakfast? Have you ever jumped out of bed in the morning excited because you knew that God was going to rain down His glory? This is how we should feel, but the truth of the matter is, God's glory terrifies most people.

At one point the people told God not to ever speak to them again. "Speak to us through Moses," they said. They didn't want Him to speak to them directly because it scared them to death (Exodus 20:19). Because of this thinking, they never entered the Holy Place.

The priests, however, were different. They couldn't wait for Moses to show them God's commands so that they might see His glory. Moses instructed them how to daily have communion with God as they ate the shewbread. He instructed them on how to offer up sacrifices of incense (praise and worship) on the golden altar and to keep oil in the lamp stand that it might burn continually from dusk until dawn.

God is showing us through the Levites that if we want to see His glory we are to become like priests: (1) We are to be obedient to His word; (2) We are to commune with him daily through prayer; (3) We are to offer up incense of praise and worship; (4) We are not to quench the Holy Spirit.

Number One Benefit of the Holy Place: His Glory

Obedience causes His Glory to appear

There will be times in your life when the Lord will ask you to do something and, like the Israelites, you might be scared to death. You will have to overcome fear and choose faith if you want His glory to appear.

The next time you feel negative peer pressure from a boyfriend or a girlfriend, remind yourself that you are a princess and you would rather have God's glory than their approval. You will be amazed as your confidence starts to build and your face begins to shine as you reject the peer pressure and listen to the Holy Spirit within you.

Be obedient when He tells you to phone a friend and say you're sorry and watch the glory of His healing.

Listen when He tells you not to date someone, as it wouldn't be God's best for you, and watch His glory as He brings a prince into your life.

Guys dig girls who hear and obey God!

Prayer Causes His Glory to Appear

According to the book of James, we don't receive our ridiculous request because we don't ask and when we do ask, we ask with the wrong motives (James 4:2-3).

I am convinced one reason so many girls never get the fairytale lifestyle they dream of is because they never thought about praying for it. Most girls I talk to have one main dream: marrying a prince and having a great family. Their biggest fear is divorce. Don't get me wrong. They have many ambitions and goals, but marriage seems to be the number one. Most of them have never thought about praying to God for their spouse. What a crazy thought—letting God pick your husband.

I took a young woman in her late twenties to breakfast one morning and I asked her, "What do you want in life?"

"I would love to be married." She said. "I'm apprehensive because I've had a few serious relationships that didn't work out. I can't seem to find a compatible mate. My parents divorced so I guess I don't know what a healthy relationship looks like." She sighed and continued, "I just want a faithful, loving, Christian man."

"Have you ever thought about praying for a spouse?" I questioned.

"I never gave it much thought," she replied.

At a small gathering this young woman addressed the crowd. "My life changed when I started praying for my spouse," she announced boldly. There was a twinkle in her eye as she smiled at me. I knew she had discovered an amazing truth—to see God's glory through prayer! Today she's happily married and the mother of twins.

A man once said to me that having a great marriage is the closest thing we have here on earth to heaven and having a bad marriage will be the closest thing we have here on earth to hell.

Praying for the man of your dreams and a great marriage is not only right, it's imperative. No matter what your age, if you are single make it your priority to start praying for your future husband. Pray that he will always love you, pray for his financial future, and pray that he will be a great father. Pray that he will be a man after God's own heart and watch God's glory fall on you.

Do you want to see His glory daily? Then get on your knees and commune with Him. Pray while you're taking the test and watch His glory appear as you start recalling the answers. Have you lost your schoolwork? Your keys? Pray and they appear supernaturally. Spend time communing with God as He has crowned you with glory (splendor) and honor (favor, beauty, Excellency).

Guys love girls who talk to God!

Praises Cause His Glory to Appear

God inhabits the praises of His people. Many of us think that the only time to praise God is in church. But one of the greatest ways to praise the Lord is by praising His great works, His creations, and we are his greatest creations.

When the Holy Spirit tells you to compliment someone, do it. When you see a girl who has the outfit on that you wanted but couldn't afford, tell her how great she looks. When you meet a stranger in the grocery store and you love her hairstyle, go tell her. If you get a great waiter, tell him (and then leave a good tip)! In praising them you are praising God, and you can expect to see His glory appear to you.

As I walked into my daughter's school to watch her basketball game, a woman stopped me and complimented me on how nice I looked and how much she loved my long, flowered coat. Her words of praise lifted me up. All I could think about as she spoke was how beautiful this woman was. She was quickly becoming my new best friend as her praises melted my heart.

Praise not only makes us feel good, it can change our lives.

Four years of high school had been difficult for Ryan. His parents' divorce had taken him by surprise his freshman year and now the girl he thought he would spend the rest of his life with, dumped him.

He slumped as he opened his locker to put his Business Math book away for the very last time. "Never again will I be an inconvenience to my dad and his new girlfriend or a hassle for my mom," he said under his breath. The loneliness, the pain of his parents' divorce, the rejection he felt from peers had finally won out. It would all be over tonight; Ryan planned on parking his car in the garage then taking his .22 pistol from underneath his car seat, placing the barrel against his temple, and pulling the trigger.

"Ryan, can I speak to you for a moment?" A gentle voice behind him said.

"What's up?" Ryan said in a distraught voice.

"Ryan, I just can't thank you enough," Andrea, a girl who was in a couple of his classes, said. "You have no idea how much you helped me in math. For weeks I've struggled with percentages and decimals but after you showed us on the board today how you came up with your answer to last night's homework, I finally got it! Have you ever thought about being a teacher?" She patted his shoulder and walked away.

"Never," he whispered as he turned and slammed his locker shut, but her encouraging words echoed in his head: (*Teacher, teacher, teacher.*)

Twenty-five years later Ryan smiles as he stands before his class and his students raise their hands and call him "teacher." "Teacher!" "Teacher!!"

There is nothing prettier than a young girl who can offer compliments and receive them gracefully with a "thank you." Trust me. It makes you beautiful, it melts God's heart and His glory, and honors are all over you.

Guys are smitten by praising words!

Worship Causes His Glory to Appear

Many times we don't worship like we should because we are afraid of what others will think. The word "worship" in Hebrew means, "to prostrate to royalty, bow down, humbly beseech, do reverence, and make to stoop."

King David's wife, Michal, criticized him for praising and worshiping the Lord in a way she didn't think was proper for a king. She said he was uncovered (naked) because he wasn't dressed in his kingly attire. In her opinion, he was behaving like an idiot as he danced, shouted, and sang unto the Lord in front of all the people. God was so upset with her for criticizing David's time of worship with Him that He cursed her and caused her to become barren (2 Samuel 6: 20-23).

For the longest time I wanted to raise my hands in church. I just wanted to be free to show my love for the Lord. My fear of what others would think kept me from expressing myself. After all, I was raised in a church where once you entered the sanctuary you weren't to say a word.

One day, I was in the front row at church with hundreds of people behind me when God said, "June, bow down before me!"

"Now, God" I whispered. "I've just overcome my fear of raising my hands and you want me to bow right here and now? Are you kidding me? People will think I'm sick or wounded!"

As the song continued, I could not stand any longer, because I knew I was disobeying God. The next thing I knew, I was on my knees worshiping the Lord. What a moment God and I had together! I became naked spiritually. I was humbly bowing before the King, sobbing, but I didn't care what others thought. I only wanted to please my Lord. His glory, His splendor, His love was upon me. Oh, what a moment!

The Bible tells us to listen to God and forget about what others think and forget about the way we were raised. "Then the King will desire our beauty; because He is our Lord, bow down to Him" (Psalm 45:10-11).

We shouldn't worry about what others think of us as we worship naked; we should be praying that God would strip them so that they might enjoy His glory!

Guys dig girls who worship naked! (Spiritually, that is!)

Faith, Obedience, Prayer, Praise, Worship, Holy Spirit, Will Cause His Glory to Appear

Sometimes faith, obedience, prayer, praise, worship, and the Holy Spirit will take us out of our comfort zones and put our reputations on the line.

It was Christmastime and I just wasn't in the mood to take a bunch of teenage mothers and their babies to camp. But out of obedience to the Lord I finally consented.

A few mentors and myself loaded six teenage mothers and their babies onto a bus and headed to Frontier Ranch, a Young Life camp in Colorado. I sat beside Collene, a fifteen-year-old girl who was three months pregnant and unmarried. We talked about the baby's father. "Will you marry him?" I questioned.

"He's married." She responded while keeping her head down. "My mother kept telling me to be nice to him. He drove me to school, I thought he loved me, but as it turned out I was the price for my mother's drugs."

I wanted to vomit. I had four daughters of my own and couldn't imagine selling one of them for drugs.

Suddenly she turned to me and said, "A demon unpacked my suitcase this morning."

I was shocked and upset. What kind of response was she expecting? Did she say all of this to upset me? As I looked into her eyes, I saw that she really believed what she'd just said. How could I, an ordinary wife and mother, deal with her emotional pain, much less demons, real or imagined? I excused myself and spent the rest of the trip talking with other girls. By the time we pulled into camp, I was mentally exhausted from all the sad stories that I had heard.

Driving into the ranch at night was mystical. Snow was lightly falling, adding beauty to the snowcapped pine trees. Our breath was visible as the cold air entered our warm lungs only to come out as steam. The dimly lit cabins looked so peaceful, so quaint. Mist from the hot spring's pool invited us in. Lit up in the center of it all was a large tennis court that held a basketball hoop at each end. Hundreds of students gathered there dressed in their winter attire. The excitement was undeniable. There was something truly divine in this place just waiting to be discovered.

Each evening the whole camp, four to five hundred students, assembled for "club talk." We worshiped, praised, and then heard the gospel of Jesus Christ. During one evening session the speaker said, "I want each of you to go spend quiet time with only God." It was a crisp night and the stars were dancing above the Rocky Mountain moonlit peaks. I shivered as I prayed for the young mothers. I began to hear the voice of the Lord. "June," He said. "I have prepared the hearts of five girls to come to Me tonight."

"Five! Lord, there are six girls," I contested as if He couldn't count! "O.K. I understand, Collene isn't ready for you," I thought.

"Tell someone what I've spoken to you," came the voice deep within my soul.

I had new leaders with me. What would they think when I told them that I had just heard from God? "What if it isn't true," I questioned myself? Oh, the kisses of betrayal were stinging me on the face like a cold, hard hailstorm. I had a choice to make: Was I going to be obedient and see the Glory of the Lord, or was the kiss of betrayal (fear) going to rule me?

When I walked into the building the first leader I came to, was a woman named Peggy Wood. I quickly explained all that the Lord had told me, wondering if she was going to check me into the mental hospital. *I hear from God and Collene sees demons; now who's crazy?*

At cabin time that night all six girls shared with the leaders how they had received the kisses of betrayal in their lives. They were left with hurt, pain, and despair. As the meeting ended, I asked, "Have any of you ever thought of giving your life to Jesus?"

They looked at me as if I'd just suggested they talk to Collene's demons.

"Okay, here's what we're going to do," I said. "Kneel in a circle and close your eyes. I'll lead you in praise and worship of the Lord. There is no pressure; this is between you and the Lord," I assured them.

Our eyes were closed; Peggy asked the girls to pray with her. "God, we know not one of us is perfect. We need you. We know that you can change our lives. Please take our sins away and become our Savior. Amen."

The door opened and closed. Had someone entered? Or had everyone left Peggy and me alone on our knees?

I slowly lifted my head and looked around. It was the most beautiful sight I've ever seen: Five teenage girls, on their knees, weeping, had just accepted Jesus as their Savior. I quickly scanned the room to see whom God had called. My eyes did a double—take; there she was, a beautiful dark-haired girl—Collene.

"Girls, this night is no accident," Peggy shared. "It is a prophecy come true." We all cried tears of joy as God's words had been fulfilled. He was real and His Glory had come upon us.

"Let's go tell somebody," one girl exclaimed.

"Let's show God love's to the girl who left," cried a softened heart.

"Let's share with the other cabins how God saved us!" another voice shouted.

The fever of excitement was exploding. The glory of the Lord was all over that camp as the word spread fast; God had spoken and five teenage moms had been saved. Glory and honor to our Lord, Amen!

God's glory didn't stop at camp: On our way home from camp Collene began witnessing to the gas station attendant.

God's glory didn't stop there: As Collene's time to deliver the baby was drawing near, her mother took her back to the Indian reservation in New Mexico. If Collene delivered the baby there, there was a good chance that that baby would stay at the reservation, because the Indians have their own laws. But God had another plan. A police officer noticed a tail-light missing on their car and pulled them over. While checking the license of her mother, the officer found that there was a warrant out for her arrest. He arrested Collene's mother on the spot and Collene was brought back to Colorado to live with a grandmother.

God's glory didn't stop there: When Collene returned to Colorado she needed to see her doctor but her grandmother didn't have a car. So she called me. While waiting for Collene at the doctor's office, God told me to take her home with me so I did. She told me she was having some pain and discomfort. I tucked her into bed like a scared two-year-old and laid my hands on her and prayed. Little did we know that she was in labor and that by the next evening she would be the mother of a beautiful baby girl named Zoe.

God's glory didn't stop there Zoe was adopted by a loving Christian couple.

God's glory didn't stop there: After being dismissed from the hospital Collene was removed from her mother's custody and placed in a strong Christian home. She was healed from seeing demons, taken off all of her psychotic drugs, and for the first time began loving herself.

God's glory didn't stop there: After graduating from high school, Collene went on to missionary college and fell in love with a wonderful young Christian man.

God's glory didn't stop there: On October 21, 2006, Collene was married and her daughter Zoë was her flower girl.

God's glory won't stop there: Collene and her husband know of God's greatness and have dedicated their lives to tell of His great glory.

When the Aaronic priests were obedient to what the Lord had told them the camp would see God's glory (Leviticus 9:23).

Perhaps those girls would have accepted Jesus as their savior on that night without my obedience, Peggy's prayer, our praise, worship, and letting the Spirit move. But the whole camp would have missed seeing His glory.

Sweet, beautiful girls, if you will learn His ways, people around you will get to see His glory. Does your family need to see His glory? Does your school?

How about your friends? Obey and watch the blessings start to fall. Choose God's side and watch everything around you change.

The Second Benefit of the Holy Place: Honor (favor, beauty)

Moses said, "If you are pleased with me, teach me your ways, so I may know you and continue to find favor with you" (Exodus 33:13).

As you learn God's ways, you will know Him better and find favor with Him. When we find favor with God, we receive special treatment.

Now don't take this wrong. We aren't supposed to be arrogant, but if we are walking with God we should expect His favor. Remember, we're royalty. I expect people to show me favor because I pray for it and because I am a princess in God's kingdom.

Recently, we booked a trip to the Magic Kingdom in Florida. I'd always dreamed of staying at the Polynesian Village. Disappointment washed over me as the lady on the phone informed me that they were sold out during our stay due to Spring Break. I begged her to re-check. Then I remembered that I'm favored, I get special benefits. So I began to pray while she looked. She returned to the phone and said, "Mrs. Fellhauer, I've been talking to our computer technician and there's a mess-up on our computer. We do have a room."

With vigor in my voice I said, "I knew it, I'm favored!"

She started laughing and said, "Do you mean to tell me your faith got you this room?"

"Yes, that's what I'm telling you," I exclaimed. My husband smiled and shook his head when I told him about the conversation.

A young woman phoned me. "We are really struggling financially," she said. "I'd like to stay home with my baby but things are so tight. I don't even have enough money for a haircut. Not to mention the fact that my husband and I would love to go on a date but can't afford it."

"You are walking with the Lord," I assured her. "God will bless you."

A few days later this young women e-mailed me.

> "Dear June,
>
> Thank you for your encouragement. God is faithful. I went to work and out of the blue, my boss gave me a fifty-dollar certificate to a hair salon. It not only paid for the haircut, it was enough for the tip. That's not all. A co-worker unexpectedly gave me two tickets to

the movies along with coupons for refreshments. I didn't even pray for popcorn. God gave me more than I expected!"

This young woman walks in the ways of God. God could hardly wait to show her favor, but He wanted her to ask. We don't have because we don't ask.

When my husband competes for a sale in his real estate business, I always believe that he will have victory. Why, because we are favored. We are heirs to the throne, and royalty gets special treatment.

If things don't turn out like I think they will, if my husband doesn't get the contract, I still know that I'm favored and God is sparing us from an unpleasant event or has something better in mind.

Start believing that the King of the Universe desires to shower you with His favor, His royal treatment. Believe that you can make the cheerleading squad, the basketball team, the debate team, be a straight "A" student, or the homecoming queen. Why? You are favored. You are a princess and it pleases the Lord when we have faith in what He says.

God says that you became His and that He adorned you with ornaments, bracelets and necklaces. He crowned you with a beautiful crown. And you are exceedingly beautiful and advanced to royalty. Your beauty is perfect because of His splendor, which He bestowed on you (Ezekiel 16:8-14).

I can see the glamour magazine headlines now! "Peasant Girl Becomes A Red-Carpet Beauty." Beauty secrets inside . . . faith, obedience, praising, praying, and worshiping brings youth and beauty to homely girl.

Few enter the Holy Place because most desire the ways of the world over the ways of God. They want to be praised more than they want to praise. They care more what man thinks than what God thinks. They trust in man more than they trust in God. Those who dare to walk in the ways of the Lord enter into the Holy Place. They will be obedient, pray, praise, and worship fervently and never look the same. They are crowned with glory and honor; they are beautiful.

Guys love beautiful girls!

Kingdom Rule # 4: Entering the Holy of Holies—Virgins (Pure Hearts)

God has created us for intense moments of personal grandeur! These moments are training for the day when we meet Him face to face.

While entering the courts takes faith and walking the ways of God allows you the honor of the Holy Place, I need to caution you before we go on. You are about to enter a no-spin zone. The Holy of Holies isn't for the weak-hearted; it's for the thrill-seekers, the risk-takers, and the lovers of God.

In the days of Moses, once a year, on the tenth day of the seventh month, The Day of Atonement, the high priest would risk his life as he went before the Lord into the Holy of Holies and offered a sacrifice that would purify all his people from their sins. If the high priest wasn't pure when he entered the Holy of Holies, he would die, because sin cannot be in the presence of God. Tradition teaches that the people would tie a rope around his ankle so that they could drag him out if he perished. There would be much soul-searching, repenting and confessing of any and all sins.

On the morning of the Day of Atonement, fear gripped his heart as the High Priest dressed in his royal robes. Nervously, he placed the last article of adornment on his head, the pure gold holy crown; there were so many lives at stake, including his own. His cotton-dry mouth made it hard to swallow. The heaving pounding of his heart made it almost impossible to breathe as he approached the veil that separated the Holy Place from the Holy of Holies. Overcoming his fear, he laid his life on the line as he lifted the cantor of incense above his head, praising, worshiping, and seeking God's will, not his own. As smoke from the cantor filled the room, supernaturally, the priest passed through the veil and into the presence of God.[1] No other moment in life would compare to this one experience—this intimacy with God.

Perhaps the Shulammite girl craves a similar experience, maybe that would explain her wanting to risk her life and make such a ridiculous request or perhaps it's love! Pure love! The Shulammite girl had fallen in love, and she was single-minded in her devotion to Solomon. Her admiration for him compels her. She desires his presence. A deep, deep longing for intimacy covers her like a warm blanket.

Dreaming about being in the arms of Solomon, awaking next to him every morning drives her. Imagining herself dressed in the garments of the queen and adorned with the crown of authority is almost more that she can stand. Her pure love for Solomon, the glory of the kingdom, and a desire deep within her soul requires her to risk her life.

As we stand at the door of the throne room our hearts will race. Our minds will spin out of control with past thoughts: "Am I pure enough? Am I beautiful

1 Dick Reuben Evangelistic Association, video series, *The Pattern for Revival*, tape *The Golden Altar*

enough? Am I young enough? Have I praised enough? Prayed enough?" Then that final voice will shout, "Don't risk your life! You'll die in there!" Most will turn and run back to the outer courts.

According to the book of Hebrews, we have a right to the throne of God. Our great high priest Jesus made us with out sin, pure virgins as He wrapped His robe of righteousness around us (Hebrews 4:16-16, Isaiah 61:10). In fact, we are to come to the throne with confidence and state our ridiculous request. Mercy and grace have been extended to us though the King's golden scepter—Jesus! (Hebrews 1:8). There is no sin that cannot be erased. Simply confess and repent, put on your royal robe, and prepare to enter.

While the Holy of Holies is available to those who have faith in Jesus, few will enter because the throne of God is a scary thought for most. It's a place where we are out of control and God is in control. It's a place where ordinary people do extraordinary things. It's a place where visions of your heart are revealed. Where you lay down your flesh and live by God's spirit. The presence of God dwells in this place.

Jesus said, "If anyone wishes to come after Me, he must deny himself, and take up his cross daily and follow Me" (Luke 9:23).

We have to die and give up our lives as we know it. We automatically think, *what a drag, I'm not giving up my great life.* Yet, we seem to miss the fact that the disciples laid their lives, their businesses, and their families down, to follow Jesus and because of that, their farms, families and brothers were increasing a hundred fold supernaturally (Mark 10:28-30). We also forget that they were experiencing miracle after miracle. Not to mention that Jesus' power had rubbed off on them and they were healing, taking control over spirits, sicknesses, and diseases (Matthew 10:1).

When God told me to write this book, fear gripped me like a barbed-wire girdle. I hadn't even written a letter in the past twenty-five years. I started dreaming that I was speaking in front of large crowds. I would wake up gasping for air. Then I realized this was my Holy of Holies. This was the calling on my life. If I was ever going to experience the supernatural power of God, I had to stop depending upon my abilities and start depending on His. But before I dared to enter, I had to check my heart and my motives. Was I pure before the Lord? I knew if I wasn't, I'd perish.

Your Holy of Holies may look different; perhaps you dream of becoming a doctor, lawyer, designer, model, engineer, missionary, or an Olympian. A voice in your head says you can't do it. You can't make the grades or afford to go to the finest colleges. You don't have enough talent.

Before you enter into your dream, you need to ask one simple question: Is your heart pure? In other words, do you have the right motives? Do you want to do it because God has placed a love there or are you doing it for you own glory, a lot of money, or recognition? If you heart is not pure, you'll die. Your dream job will become your nightmare position.

If your heart is pure, stop depending on your resources. Lay it down and let God worry about it. He's calling you to virgin experiences. While the word "virgin" means to "separate" (from her privacy), it has another meaning in Hebrew: "something kept out of sight, veiled." For those with a pure heart, He wants to bring the veil of your soul down and show you something that is so big, so grand; it has been out of sight. He's saved this secret just for you. He knows it's bigger than you. It's more than you ever dreamed of, and as you step closer it will scare you to death. You may have an idea of what your dream looked like, but now He wants to reveal it to you. He wants you to be so intimate, so dependent on Him that His power rubs off on you. He wants to answer your ridiculous request and give you moments of grandeur as you overcome your fears and live the dreams that He has unveiled to you.

I searched high and low to give you an example of what it might look like to enter into the Holy of Holies right here on earth. I thought about Miss America receiving her crown, the Olympian receiving his gold medal. Perhaps a mother giving birth would suffice. But then I watched a young man named Owen Washburn ride into his Holy of Holies.

The fringe of his leather chaps swished and the clanging of his spurs made a statement as Owen Washburn paraded through the tunnel and into the arena on the night of March 25, 2000 in Albuquerque, New Mexico.

He zipped up his black protective jacket and jammed his mouthpiece onto his teeth, his final act before climbing aboard a 2000-pound beast called "Promise Land."

As he settled on the monster, he pulled up the slack of his resin-coated rope. He wrapped the rope securely around his hand, tying himself to the bull. Anxiously he waited for the stock contractor to tighten the flank strap.

His heart raced. His life was on the line. Flashbacks taunted him. A slow-motion movie played over and over again in his head. Last night, this very animal had cruelly twisted and turned with rage, launching his friend Glen Keeley into the arena's manure-packed dirt. As a warrior pierces the heart of his enemy with his sword, the beast drove his hind hooves into Glen's chest, killing him.

The rattle of the gate brought Owen back to the present. He nodded. The gate opened and the violent dance began. It was man versus beast where eight seconds would seem like an eternity.

The beast soared out of the gate. He maliciously whipped and spun the rider, trying to throw him off.

Flopping like a rag doll, Owen fought back. He extended his legs and planted his spurs into the side of the beast, using every muscle he had to center himself on the wild animal.

Promised Land spiraled out of control. Snot flew through the air as the creature snorted.

With four seconds gone, the crowd rose to its feet, shouting, cheering, raising hands, and hoping for a miracle. Could Owen overcome the beast that had taken the life of his friend? His strength was no contender for the bull. But deep inside him was something supernatural, a presence of greatness—faith.

As the buzzer sounded, Owen dismounted in victory. The crowd erupted. Tears of joy, exuberance, and accomplishment filled the stadium. The cowboys behind the dusty chutes choked with emotion as they wiped the muddy tears from their checks. Redemption was paid for. What a moment of glory for Owen Washburn as he was crowned champion bull rider on that bittersweet night!

A bull rider risks his life night after night for the love, the rush, the rage, and the glory. Spending eight seconds in the presence of greatness outweighs the fear of death.[2]

Dear young, beautiful, girls, redemption had been paid. Risk your life, enter the throne room, hear His voice, and see His dreams for your life and the mysteries of God unveiled to you. Make your ridiculous requests. Then experience His extraordinary grandeur as you soak in the glory of His presence. Eight seconds in His presence outweighs the fear of death! Amen!

Kingdom Challenge:

Before you go on to another chapter, I have a request for you. On the Day of Atonement, the people would humble themselves and go before the Lord. They did this by fasting and praying. I challenge you to fast from all foods from sunup until sundown. You may drink water and juice. Every time you want food, I want you deny your flesh and ask God to show you His will for your life. I

2 Technical advice from my husband Jay (former bull rider)

want you to see that you can overcome your flesh, you can say "no" to it, but it takes work. Praise Him, thank Him, and dance with Him. Pray for a clean heart and be prepared to enter into the Holy of Holies.

Today's One-Liner: ....Jesus, Our Redeemer!
Clue for living "Happily Ever After" .... Hebrew 11:6

> *"And without faith it is impossible to please Him, for he who comes to God must believe that He is and that He is a rewarder of those who seek Him."*

Kiss of Love:...Faith
Kiss of Betrayal:.. Fear

Chapter Four

She's in Love with the Boy!

"The King has brought me into his chambers"
Song of Solomon 1:4

Dating! It really hasn't changed much in the last 3000 years, unless you are Princess Aurora snoozing under a curse! Dating is time spent in the wilderness with the one with whom you might enter into the promised land of marriage. Go spend some time out in the real world with him. Set your tent next to his and learn all that you can. If you can't get along with him in the boondocks (the dating period), you certainly don't want to live with him for the rest of your life.

Upon receiving a ridiculous request from a peasant girl, I can imagine Solomon response, *"Bring that crazy Shulammite girl to the palace," he orders, delighted that all of his wooing and charm is finally paying off.*

"What, a date with the king? He's asked me to the palace!" she exclaims. I picture chills run up and down her spine as she disguises her enormous smile with her hands. For a brief moment the world is perfect and then reality kicks in. What will I wear? What will I say? How will I do my hair?

Insecurity is easy to spot in our own lives, as we get ready for the big date, especially if we are going into his territory. The closet is bare and every single outfit is lying on the bed. We try on each piece two or three times but nothing seems to fit just right or looks perfect. We parade to the mirror with hopes that something about our body has miraculously changed from our previous appearance five seconds ago. We stand in front of the mirror with our shoulders back and our chests puffed out. Then while holding our breath and making a slight turn to the side, we suck our stomachs in. Our final fitness move is to flex our butt muscles. If we can only stay like this all night, we may pull this two-sizes-too-small outfit off. Take advice from someone who's been there: Choose the comfortable outfit and be yourself.

Here's the irony of it all: We aren't dressing for the guy we are dating; we are dressing for the surrounding territory (other girls). We want to make sure we are not inferior to anyone. Our Shulammite girl shares in our feelings as well. Let's watch as she enters into his territory.

A crack emerges between the magnificent doors of the palace as the guards thrust them open for the visitor. There is a hush in the Holy Place as all eyes focus on the arrival of the Shulammite girl. Her eyes are wide open and her stomach flips as she scans the exquisite room. Every girl in the palace seems to be dressed in the latest fashions and they are all made-up like they've just jumped off the cover page of the new "Seventeen" magazine. They are beautiful.

The Shulammite girl's comfort level hits an all-time low as her walls of defense reach their summit. Her defense begins: "I'm black but lovely, O daughters of Jerusalem, like the tents of Kedar, like the curtains of Solomon. Do not stare at me because I am swarthy, for the sun has burned me. My mother's sons were angry with me; they made me caretaker of the vineyards, but I have not taken care of my own vineyard" (Song of Solomon 1:5-6).

Can't you just picture her attitude? I imagine her pointing her finger and shaking her head as she states, "Don't you stare at me, girl! I'll whop you up side of the head. I might be black, my skin might look like leather, but I have a heart of gold. You have no right to judge me. You don't know what I've been through!"

Insecurity! It hits us when we are out of our comfort zone. It makes us say and think the most bizarre things. Instead of being comfortable with who we are, we start making excuses for who we are not, or we start blasting others for who they are (or who they are not). Our mouths launch derogatory words like missiles honing in on a target: ditsy cheerleaders, dumb jocks, nerd herd, and control freak. Mission accomplished. Wound before being wounded. Reject before being rejected. But there is a hole in our hearts the size of the Grand Canyon because we long to be accepted and yet worry about being unwanted.

Solomon appears on the scene and her language changes: "Tell me, O you whom my soul loves, where do you pasture your flock, where do you make it lie down at noon?" (Song of Solomon 1:7). Shazaam! She goes through a metamorphosis in the presence of the one she loves. Do you see what's going on here? Insecurity makes her (us) ugly, nasty, and mean. Love makes her (us) nice and attractive.

Her first question to Solomon is, "Where do you pasture your flock, where do you hang out?" We all know what happens when we become interested in a guy. We become charming and our hangout spots change. We now are being spotted at soccer games that we never attended before. As if through supernatural powers, we become experts on the rules of basketball, or football apparel is our new favorite clothing. Everywhere he is, we seem to appear. Then it happens, someone is onto us. When confronted with the title of "stalker," we deny every offense.

Why do we deny the fact that we want to be special in someone's life? Is it we are afraid he won't feel the same way and we will be humiliated? Perhaps we feel this person is out of our league so we just toy with the idea, hoping that we might be the next Cinderella. We're never really honest about our feelings because somehow this protects us. Right?

The Shulammite girl struggles with the same problem. Fearing that she may not be attractive to Solomon, she activates her defensive wall again and claims that she isn't that interested in Solomon. "For why should I be like one who veils herself beside the flock of your companions?" (Song of Solomon 1:7). The women who veiled themselves and hung out around the shepherds' tents were considered prostitutes or groupies if you will. She tells him she won't be his groupie, his cheerleader at the game, or part of his clique. In a roundabout way, she's throwing out bait to see where she stands with him. She's trying to tell him that she wants a personal relationship with him but she will not become like the other girls, nor will she compete for him. She may have some insecurities but she will not lower her standards to date the guy of her dreams.

In high school I started dating the lead singer and guitar player of a country western band called "The Good, The Bad, and The Ugly." My dad had become a fan of his music and insisted that he and my mom take me to his next gig. Sitting in a smoke-infested bar on a Friday night with your parents isn't exactly heaven—but watching the love of your life on stage is.

I really believed that I was the only one in the room who was "crazy in love" with this guy. My vision of romance was coming true as he took a break and made his way to my table. I envisioned him coming over to me, whisking me into his muscle-bound body and kissing me as if to say, "This is my woman."

I was knocked back to my senses as a swarm of beautiful girls encircled him on the dance floor. "He'll push through the crowd, longing to see me," I thought. Not! He flirted with them. He made sure that I could see that he was quite the attraction. Then he moseyed over to my table.

I was devastated, hurt, jealous, and furious. I felt inferior to all those young, beautiful women. Insecurity ruled and I was about to get ugly. "I won't share you with anyone. It's me or them," I said with all the confidence I could muster. *I will not be a groupie, I will not compete for your attention, and I will not follow you around like a puppy on a leash.*

I was in love with the guy but I wasn't about to become like one of those girls and competing with them was not going to be on my to do list.

The Shulammite girl didn't want to compete with other women for Solomon. I didn't want to compete for my love, and God doesn't want to compete for you! He doesn't want you to be a number in a church pew or a voice in the crowd yelling, "Go, God!" He doesn't want to be second in line to your sport activities, your grades, your friends, or anything else. I ask girls all the time: show me your bank statement, the materials you read and your old school planner and I will tell you if God is your number one heartthrob. He wants you to be intimate with Him. Plainly, He tells us, "You shall have no other gods before Me" (Exodus 20:3). He's jealous over us and won't share our love with anyone or anything. He also will never change to be part of the crowd. It's His way of giving us our first clue to successful dating. Dating Clue # 1: If you are always competing for your love's attention, or need to become like someone else, run that young man off!

The daughters of Jerusalem (girls in the palace) are taken back by the Shulammite girl; they can't believe that she doesn't know how much Solomon loves her. They are amazed that she's insecure. They refer to her as "most beautiful among women" (Song of Solomon 2:8). They are saying to her, girl, it's you he's in love with, not us. We're his best friends and he's told us how he feels about you! If you don't believe how beautiful you are, go spend some time with Solomon and realize how smitten he is with you, see the way he looks at you, they advise her (Song of Solomon1:8).

The dating stage is a wonderful scene. While it can have its awkward moments, it's also a fun time spent in the open with friends and family playing Monopoly, enjoying school events, and getting to know one another. It is not a time for the backseat of a car.

God tells us to "behave properly as in the day, not in carousing and drunkenness, not in sexual promiscuity and sensuality, not in strife and jealousy. But put on the Lord Jesus Christ and make no provision for the flesh in regard to its lusts" (Romans 13:14). In other words, stay in the light, around people so that you don't set yourself up for failure. God is warning us about the guy who is always trying to get you alone with him. Dating Clue # 2: If your love is always trying to alienate you from other people, run that young man off!

Have you ever been around a guy who is trying to compliment you but the more he talks the more timid you become? You aren't sure what he's trying to say so you assume the worst?

Solomon begins their relationship with these very words. "To me, my darling, you are like my mare among the chariots of Pharaoh. Your cheeks are lovely with ornaments. Your neck with strings of beads" (Song of Solomon 1:9).

If a guy said this to me, my first reaction would be *I must be fat*! Mares have huge thighs and they eat all the time. I would envision my cheeks looking like puffy round Christmas tree ornaments and my neck resembling something like Wilma Flintstone's pearl necklace. Everything about this statement says FAT to a woman!

One of the problems with the human race is that girls and guys don't think alike. While we might take offense at Solomon's comments, he is actually giving her a huge compliment. He loves horses. In fact he had 40,000 stalls of them (I King 4:26). His mare was imported from Egypt (2 Chronicles 1:16). They were priceless to him and so is she. He's comparing her to fine jewels. She's a real find, a great catch.

God has been complimenting us for years. He calls us His sheep. While I personally think sheep are some of the dumbest animals on the planet, God knows that they are of great worth to a shepherd. He calls us His children, praising us since there is nothing more precious than a child. God compliments us throughout the Bible because He's giving us another clue to a great relationship. Dating Clue # 3: If your love cannot compliment you, run that young man off!

While dining together, her perfume gives forth its fragrance. The Shulammite girl comments, "My beloved is to me a pouch of myrrh which lies all night between my breasts" (Song of Solomon 12-14). Now if Solomon doesn't get in touch with how a woman communicates, he's going to get a very wrong signal. She is simply returning his compliment with one of her own. The pouch between her breasts is filled with very expensive perfume. They didn't bathe much in those days so a breathing bottle of perfume was very valuable. They never took it off. She's trying to tell Solomon how much he means to her. They are considering each other's feelings, complimenting each other and having great regard for one another. This brings us to our next clue. Dating Clue # 4: If there is not mutual respect in the dating stage, run that young man off!

Their relationship goes deeper as Solomon states, "How beautiful you are, my darling, how beautiful you are. Your eyes are like doves" (Song of Solomon 1:15). Soft are the eyes of the dove. They have no peripheral vision, signifying singleness of vision. They mate for life. He's conveying that he appreciates that she looks at him in a gentle way, not with an evil eye. We women can give "a look" that can send a laser beam into a man's soul and pulverize it. Solomon appreciates her gentleness and that she only has eyes for him.

Again the girl responds with a compliment. "How handsome you are, my beloved and so pleasant" (Song of Solomon 1:15-16). These two are very playful, and she is expressing that he is fun to be with; he's her new best friend. They are telling us that dating shouldn't be a grind or a chore.

If you are always fighting in the dating stage there's a problem. Many couples think that once they're married all the bickering will go away. It will only get worse. It's like initials carved in the tree; the fights only get bigger. Praise God for showing us this hint. Dating Clue # 5: If he isn't pleasant to be around, run that young man off!

The zeal of their relationship begins to heat up as they are in an outdoor setting. Gazing into his eyes she passionately proclaims, "Our couch is luxuriant. The beams of our houses are cedars, our rafters, cypresses. I'm the rose of Sharon. The lily of the valleys" (Song of Solomon 1:17-2:1).

She is describing this outdoor scenery like a palace and she is the queen. She's gone from an ugly, unsure peasant girl to the "lily of the valleys." She's no longer worried about being a groupie (lilies); she's his one and only (lily). She sees herself as beautiful, "the rose of Sharon," not swarthy. What's the secret? What caused the transformation?

She's hanging around a different crowd. She's not in the vineyard hanging with grumbling, dissatisfied people who are telling her that she's destined to be a peasant all her life. She's hanging with the king and he thinks she's beautiful. He's affirming her. "Like a lily among the thorns, so is my darling among the maidens" (Song of Solomon 2:2). She knows that the daughters of Jerusalem were right; she is the one he loves. She starts trusting in what Solomon says and seeing herself through his eyes, not through the eyes of others.

God shouts through His scripture how beautiful we are, but until we start trusting in what He says and start seeing ourselves through the eyes of Christ we will always be just insecure peasant girls. If you see yourself as ugly, maybe it's time to hang around another crowd. Go find God's friends and see if He's been talking about you. Then take heart to clue number six. Dating Clue # 6: If he can't see your beauty, run that young man off!

Do you really appreciate the guy you hang out with? Is he one in a million or is he just ordinary? The Shulammite girl has found a rare catch and she describes him as an "apple tree among the trees of the forest" (Song of Solomon 2:3). How many apple trees do you find in a forest; very few, if any. That is how exceptional Solomon is compared to other young men. "In his shade I took great delight and sat down, and his fruit was sweet to my taste" (Song of Solomon 2:3). In the shade of his arms she was protected and loved. His fruit was satisfying to her.

In Galatians five verse twenty-two there are nine fruits of the Spirit: love, joy, peace, patience, kindness, goodness, faithfulness, gentleness, and self-control. The Shulammite girl is complimenting Solomon's great character. If you find an apple tree out in the middle of the forest with these fruits, you run and get a bushel basket and gather in as much as you can! God is sharing a big secret with us: eat fruit, gather fruit, enjoy fruit, and bring it home. Dating Clue #7: If your young man has great fruit, bring him home to your momma!

Not only is the Shulammite girl giving him accolades for his fine fruit, she is rejoicing over the fact that he has brought her to his banquet hall, and his banner over her is love (Song of Solomon 2:4).

After a battle, you would see banners with the names of the twelve tribes on them: Reuben, Manasseh, Asher, Simean, Judah, and so forth. When the troops staggered in, they would stand under their tribe's banner so that they could regroup, see who belonged to whom, and find out who was missing.

In a sense, Solomon took the Shulammite girl to the Olive Garden for dinner and everyone there could see that his banner over her was love by the way he treated her. He pulled out her chair, spoke kindly to her, held her hand, and was interested in their conversation. It was obvious how much these two loved each other and he wanted her to be with him.

Our girlfriends are very good at regrouping troops. It's easy for them to see what banner is over our head. Sometimes the banner isn't love, it's "take for granted," "user," "abuser," or "loser." If you're not sure what banner you stand under, ask your friends and then praise God for giving you the banner as a sign for a healthy relationship! Dating Clue # 8: If his banner over you is love, bring that boy home to your momma!

Wining and dining at the Olive Garden was magnificent but it didn't completely satisfy the Shulammite. She wanted dessert. "Sustain me with raisin cakes; refresh me with apples, because I am lovesick" (Song of Solomon 2:5).

Raisin cakes were believed to be an aphrodisiac (something arousing sexual desire). When King David brought the ark of God back from captors, "He blessed the people and distributed to everyone of Israel both man and women to everyone a loaf of bread and a portion of meat and a raisin cake" (I Chronicles 16:3). May I suggest to you that he was advising them to go have pleasure and fulfill the covenant?

Our Shulammite is hinting that she is ready for love, his love.

Oftentimes, when we date, we fall head over heels in love with someone. Our hormones get in the way of our brains. We think we are ready for a sexual experience, so we venture into the wilderness away from protection to be alone with the man we love.

As our couple leaves the restaurant, love and lust mix like a tangled rope. Who can sort it out? They choose to be alone; temptation is lurking at their door. No one is watching as she states, "Let his left hand be under my head and his right hand embrace me" (Song of Solomon 2:6). The only way to have his hand "under" her head is if they are lying down. She wants to be in a horizontal position snuggling with Solomon. Her words and her actions cry out that she is full of sexual desire. She wants to give herself to him.

Sweet girls, the way this Shulammite girl feels is natural. God gave us these feelings and emotions. We were created to give ourselves away. These emotions will make us great lovers to our husbands and great mothers to our children one day as we give ourselves to them. Yet, these emotions have strict boundaries, and it is at this point in our lives that Satan will plant the sexual kiss of betrayal right on our lips. He will use every lie and situation possible to trip us up. He knows how weak our flesh is and therefore baits us through our emotions. He loves when we watch a movie that gives us the idea that it's okay to have sex before marriage or look at porn sites and magazines that excite our senses. He wants us to fail; sexual sins have ruined many lives and nations!

Adultery and fornication are strictly forbidden in scripture (Exodus 20:14, I Corinthians 6:9, Hebrews 13:4). Adultery is extramarital sex or voluntary sexual relations between a married person and somebody other than his or her spouse. Fornication is any kind of sex outside of marriage.

God tells us that when a couple has sex they become one (Genesis 2:24). Something spiritual happens during sex, and our souls are connected to the person we are having sex with (I Corinthians 6:16-17). Satan knows this and would love for us to be connected to tons of people, especially his people, so that he can get a foothold in our lives.

I write with authority on this subject, because this kiss almost ruined my live.

Perhaps I thought I was shielded from the sexual kiss of betrayal because of my Christian faith, but somehow it penetrated my armor. I wasn't trained in hormone warfare and my hormones were working overtime.

On the outside, I was an all-American Christian girl, a decent student, a good athlete, funny, and popular. But on the inside, I was wrestling with self-image, hormones, and weight. My biggest bout was God's ways versus the world's standards. "He (God) has become old-fashioned, just trying to keep me from having fun," I reasoned.

I had to justify my new way of living. *After all I'm in love with the band guy, right? It isn't wrong when you really love someone, is it?* This way of thinking led me into premarital sex and it was exciting! I'm not going to lie to you. There was something stimulating about planning the next rendezvous. The lying, the sneaking, the challenge of not getting caught; I was like a bank robber planning his next heist. But when the high was over, I was always filled with guilt.

I remember weekend after weekend praying to God: "Please forgive me. I won't do it again." This repentance would last only until the hormones kicked in and I found myself back in the arms of my love.

Thinking that I couldn't stop, I took the next step: birth control pills. The nurse at Planned Parenthood instructed me on how to take them and how they worked. She informed me that if and when I wanted to have children, it could take up to three months for the effect of the pills to get out of my system.

I took the nurse's word for it. I intended to be faithful to Jay while I was away at college, so why put chemicals into my body? I decided to stop taking the pills two months before I set off for Augustana College—two states away.

The nights cooled as autumn approached. The fall semester of college was only a few weeks away, and I was busy gathering decorations for my dorm room. Sioux Falls, South Dakota was a long way from Fowler, Colorado. I was nervous and not feeling so well. On the surface, I was afraid of being homesick and lovesick. Yet, deep within my soul, I was struggling with a much bigger issue. I had just received the news from the clinic. I was pregnant.

In a daze, my life passed before me. I had been caught and would spend the next eighteen years as a prisoner on house arrest. Somehow I had missed the Sunday school lesson that taught sin was only fun for a season (Hebrews 11:25). Thoughts whirled inside my head. Maybe I could escape. I could have an abortion or just go to college and give it up for adoption. No one would find out. I was so alone, so afraid. I needed to tell someone, but whom?

Options kept running through my head as I began to pack my things for college. My bedroom was a memorial to myself. On the dresser were my trophies from sports: Softball MVP, Outstanding senior Athlete, Four-year Varsity Letter for volleyball and basketball. *How could I have gone from all of this to where I am?* I began to cry.

My bedroom door opened and there standing tall was the lead singer, Jay. "Your mother said I might find you in here. Are you all right?" he said.

While trying to catch my breath, I cried, "I don't know what to do. I'm pregnant." I sobbed as he held me in his arms. His firm hug assured me that this wasn't all about me, it was about us, and there was a baby to think of.

"Will you go for a walk with me?" Jay requested. We walked to the elementary school and he began to gently push me on the swing.

"Some of my greatest memories are on this playground," He said.

I realized that both of our dreams and lives were on the line.

Ever so smoothly he stopped the swing and turned me to him. With tears in his eyes he said, "I can't think of any other place that I would rather propose to my wife. June, will you marry me?"

His response and his love brought me to my knees, a place of repentance. I knew my childhood was over, but somehow I knew my life wasn't ruined. I no longer desired the ways of the world. I had been given a second chance and I wanted to enter the Holy Place and learn to walk with God.

Have you ever been kissed with the sexual kiss of betrayal? If you have, I want you to go get a warm, soapy washcloth and I want you to wash the kiss of betrayal off of your face. Take it to the base of the cross (your wastebasket will work) and throw it away. Kneel before Jesus and tell Him all about it. He is going to take you in His arms, hold you tight, and give you the kiss of love. He will heal you, protect you, provide for you, and be intimate with you.

Solomon's response to thc Shulammite girl was similar. He didn't call the Shulammite a trashy, peasant girl when she proclaimed her feelings for him. His response was full of love "I adjure you, O daughters of Jerusalem, by the gazelles or by the hinds of the field, that you do not arouse or awaken my love until she pleases" (Song of Solomon 2:7). He's telling her that he loves her so much that he doesn't want to defile her. He asks his close friends (daughters of Jerusalem) to hold them accountable for their actions, to keep them sure-footed, pure until marriage.

Solomon knew his covenant with God. He knew that if he had sex with her before marriage he would break his covenant. He desperately wanted her, but if they were going to have the blessings of God, it was his job to keep her pure until marriage. Have you ever heard of anything more romantic? I believe it's time that we start looking for a young man who abides by clue number nine. Dating Clue # 9: If you're dating a guy who wants to keep you pure, bring that young man home to your momma!

Solomon is falling more in love with the Shulammite girl every day. He can't wait until the workday is over and he can see her again. "Cancel all of my meetings, tell the boys I can't play poker tonight," I imagine he tells his secretary. He can't concentrate, he can't eat, he can't live another minute without her and she loves it! (Song of Solomon 2:8-9)

In the middle of the night he appears at her window. On bended knee he takes her hand and whispers, "Arise, my daring, my beautiful one, and come along. For behold, the winter is past, the rain is over and gone. The flowers have already appeared in the land; the time has arrived for pruning the vines, and the voice of the turtledove has been heard in our land. The fig tree has ripened its figs and the vines in blossom have given forth their fragrance. Arise, my darling, my beautiful one, and come along!" (Song of Solomon 2:10-13). Their season of dating has passed. Solomon is head over heels in love as he proposes to this amazing, beautiful girl.

Before she can answer, he shares his fantasies with her: I can't wait for us to have our own home where you feel safe and loved; I can't wait to see your body, to wake up next to you every day for the rest of our lives and hear your voice (Song of Solomon 2:14).

He wants their love to be so pure that he says, "Let's catch the foxes, the little foxes that are ruining the vineyards, while our vineyards are in blossom" (Song of Solomon 2:15). He refers to their bodies as vineyards. He is cautioning her that they need to catch every little thing that would cause them to stumble sexually: passionate kissing, petting, time alone in the wilderness. He wants to keep the vineyard free from pests especially while they are in blossom, their most beautiful state. He knows that if the foxes eat the blossoms of the dating season there will be no fruit in the fall (marriage). He doesn't want to ruin this love affair; it's so beautiful.

The metaphor Solomon gives her pertains to the seasons in our lives. If we don't protect the blossoms (sexual purity, focus on goals, self-confidence) in the season of high school we won't have the fruit (purity, good grades, good self-esteem) for college. If I had caught the little foxes they wouldn't have been able to ruin the next season of my life, which was college. If you are in middle school you will want to catch the little foxes like jealousy, bitterness, and gossip, so that they don't ruin the fall fruit: having an amazing time in high school with great friends.

The amazing thing about God is that He keeps bringing new seasons. If we've had one bad season it doesn't mean that it has to ruin the rest of our lives. Amen!

Solomon's proposal is finished, his heart is on the line, he's played all of his cards, and his head is on the chopping block. Will she say yes or break his heart?

As I write this, I'm envisioning a 21-year-old army boy dressed in camouflage on his knees in an airport reading these very lines that Solomon wrote to my daughter, Jerrilyn. She had no idea what awaited her as she stepped off the plane and into a muggy Georgia airport.

Brandon had called and asked for my advice so I knew what was going to take place. He had also asked permission from her father. Jay's last words to a very nervous Brandon were, "I hope she says yes!"

It was the moment the Shulammite had been waiting for; her ridiculous request had been answered. "Draw me after you and let us run together!" Make me your possession, precious, prize. The Shulammite girl could hardly shout it loud enough as her lungs exploded. "My beloved is mine and I am my beloved!" (Song of Solomon 2:16). She said yes!

"The king has brought me into his chambers." She is worthy, secure, protected and provided for. "Women libbers" or feminists would be screaming at this, but we should be rejoicing, since it's a perfect picture of what happens when we say, "yes" to Christ. We, too, are worthy, secure, protected and provided for. We are betrothed to the one whom our souls love. Amen!

Kingdom Challenge:

Before you dance into the next chapter and start reading about engagement, I want to ask you something: Have you looked for love in all the wrong places? Is there something really missing in your life that you've been trying to fill with so many other things like money, boyfriends, sports, academics, but nothing fulfills the void? You desire intimacy but it feels so shallow. The treasure you are looking for is the covenant; A contract between you and God. There's only One that can fulfill the requirement of the deed. His name is Jesus. He is so crazy nuts in love with you that He gave His life on the cross so that you might have salvation (salvation is from the Greek word soteria, which means, "wholeness, deliverance, victory, prosperity, health and welfare" *blueletterbible.*

org). The only way to receive it is to believe it in your heart and confess it with your mouth that Jesus Christ is Lord (Romans 10:8-13). If you desire Jesus, will you pray with me?

Jesus, I believe you are the Son of God. I believe that I've sinned and your life is the penalty for that sin. I believe that you sacrificed your life on Calvary that I might have salvation and eternity with you. Please come into my heart and be intimate with me. Please forgive me of my sins. Teach me the ways of the covenant that I might live my life with blessings and not curses; that I might bring glory to your name. AMEN!

If you prayed that pray with your whole heart, believing every word you said. Then you are betrothed to the One whom your soul loves, Jesus Christ. I want you to find a ring and wear it on you left ring finger. This ring is a reminder that you are betrothed to the one whom your soul loves; wear this ring until it is replaced by the ring of your earthly prince.

Today's One-liner:..Jesus "My Beloved"
Clue for living "Happily Ever After":.............................. Song of Solomon 2:4

"He has brought me to his banquet hall, and his banner over me is love."

Kiss of Love:...I'm Loved
Kiss of Betrayal:... I'm Unloved

Chapter Five

Betrothed

"My Beloved Is Mine, and I Am His"
Song of Solomon 2:16

Through Song of Solomon we've seen that dating requires time, respect, communication, admiration, and a lot of self-control. We've witnessed a beautiful relationship unfold as Solomon asked the Shulammite girl to marry him and with much excitement she accepted his proposal.

In this chapter we are going to see what the Shulammite girl was entitled to when she said yes to Solomon's proposal. We are going to gain knowledge of what we are entitled to when we accept Jesus as our groom. In order for us to grasp this, we need to understand the ancient Jewish (Hebrew) marriage ceremony, as both grooms, Jesus and Solomon, were Hebrews. This wedding ceremony consisted of two main parts: *erusin,* betrothal or engagement and *nusuin,* the ceremony of matrimony.

Choosing the Bride

Had Solomon's father had been alive he would have acted in his son's best interest in choosing a bride for Solomon. If the son were old enough, perhaps, they would confer together.

Ketubah

Once the bride was selected, Solomon and his father would make a covenant or contract promise called a *ketubah*. The *ketubah* was a two-sided agreement; I will up hold my end, you will up hold your end. According to the Jewish customs, the groom had to promise three things in the *ketubah*: protection, provision, and pleasure such as sexual pleasure, intimacy (Exodus 21:10).

Jesus and His father put together a covenant or *ketubah* before the foundation of the world was created. Jesus asked His father if you could be His bride, He chose you way before you ever laid eyes on Him (Ephesians 1:4).

Accept or Reject?

According to tradition, once the *ketubah* had been prepared Solomon would then go to the bride's family and present it.

Imagine the richest and wisest king that the world had ever known, along with all of his bodyguards riding up to the house of the peasant girl on their magnificent steeds.

I can just see the Shulammite's mother throwing misplaced sandals under the old couch trying to tidy up the place before the king's entrance. She wrings her hands in her apron as she answers the door. All of her brothers (since there is no father) are called in from the fields, because king Solomon has brought important news.

"Please sit at our table," invites one brother.

Another brother offers hospitality as he pours Solomon a cup of wine. The splinter-infested table pokes Solomon's legs as he sits before the family. Solomon unrolls the scroll and presents his *ketubah*.

"I've come to ask for your daughter's hand in marriage. I offer her provision, (the wealth of the kingdom), along with protection (the finest body guards of the palace) and at the appropriate time, intimacy," he states. A tingle runs through his body, knowing how much he desires to be with the Shulammite girl.

A hush comes over the room. The family can either accept the ketubah or reject it but they cannot change it (Galatians 3:15). If they agree to his proposal, the final decision is up to the Shulammite girl; if she accepts, she will lift her cup of wine and drink as a sign of acceptance.

Can you fathom her handing the paper back to him and just walking off, implying that she doesn't want him or anything that he has to offer? Only a foolish girl or one that is in love with someone else would reject this amazing offer from the king.

At this point in the proposal, most likely Solomon's palms become clammy, beads of sweat threaten to drip from his forehead, and butterflies flutter in his stomach. It's excruciating for him to wait and see whether or not she drinks from the cup.

With all eyes on her the Shulammite girl brings the cup to her lips and takes her first sip. The first part of the marriage *ketubah* is complete. She and Solomon are now in covenant with one another. They are legally married in all aspects except for the physical consummation of marriage. She is entitled to his checking account, his credit cards, and her social status has been dramatically elevated. She has worth, protection, and provision.

Jesus, "The King of Kings," made this very covenant with His disciples and us while sitting at the table on the night of the Passover meal. He said, "I've come to give you a new covenant" (Matthew 26:28, Hebrews 12:24).

After offering His *ketubah,* Jesus went to the garden to pray. His hands were clammy, and beads of sweat dripped off of His head as He agonized over us. (*Will they drink from the cup? Will they accept the protection, provision, and passion I offer?*)

"Drink from it, all of you; for this is My blood of the covenant, which is poured out for many for forgiveness of sins" (Matthew 26:27-28). Jesus offered the disciples and us all that the Kingdom has. Who would turn it down; maybe an idiot or one not in love with Jesus? At this very point Judas excused himself and left the table before drinking the wine (John 13:27).

As we partake of that cup during communion, it's a reminder to us that we have accepted Christ's *ketubah*, which includes all of his promises, protection, and love.

Price

Before Solomon leaves her house he pays a price *mohar* to show the family he's serious. According to tradition, Solomon probably left articles of silver and gold, camels, donkeys, and other precious possessions (Genesis 24:53).

Jesus could have paid with gold or silver as all the riches, greatness, power and glory of the heavens and the earth are His (1 Chronicles 29:11-12). But He chose to give us His best by giving up His life on the cross to free us.

Promise of Return

After Solomon gives his *mohar* he makes a speech of promise. He promises the bride that he will come back to claim her as soon as he prepares a place for her to live.

Bridal Chamber

Solomon leaves the girl's home and starts to prepare a bridal chamber or a *huppah*, (house), for his bride. Their house is to be built onto his father's house. Lucky for the Shulammite girl her house will be built onto or within the Kings Palace.

A man cannot go back for the bride until the bridal chamber is complete and his father approves it. This may take some time if he's a slow carpenter or can't afford any help.

In Jesus' speech of promise he said, "In my Father's house are many mansions; if it were not so, I would have told you; for I go to prepare a place for you. If I go and prepare a place for you, I will come again and receive you to Myself, that where I am, there you may be also" (John 14:2-3).

I'm really excited what my heavenly *huppah* is going to look like. The scriptures tell us that God will give us the desires of our hearts. Most of us have no idea what our hearts desire. I realized this after we built our home. My husband teased me about having color issues due to the fact I had a hard time choosing paint colors, fabrics, furniture and anything else that was going to be around for a while. I wasn't really sure that I'd love it and I knew that I would have to live with it for a long time.

Jesus knows our desires and our style. He knows what we are going to love. He's gone to prepare a place that is going to blow our minds! I can't wait to walk into my *huppah* and see the colors, fabrics, textures, and design! Call me crazy, but I'm jazzed about my mansion!

Mikveh

After the groom leaves and sometime before the wedding, the bride takes a special bath as part of the ceremonial cleansing. It's called a *mikveh*. It represents that she is going from her old life of being single into her new life of marriage. The Shulammite girl must bathe in "living water" like a rain shower, a river, or the special *mikveh* pool.

We are to do the same thing after we accept Christ. We call this ceremony baptism. Being immersed into water represents we die to our old ways (our single life) and come up cleansed and new (the first stage of marriage to Christ).

Gift

While away working on the bridal chamber, Solomon sends the Shulammite gifts. The gifts are to remind the bride of her groom and how much he loves her. These were not shabby gifts. They were silver, gold, clothing, and so forth (Genesis 24:53).

Christ has been sending us gifts: gifts of healing, miracles, prophecy, various kinds of tongues, interpretations of tongues, words of wisdom, words of knowledge, and faith (I Corinthians 12:7-11). How sad that most of us don't even know about these gifts, much less unwrap and use them.

Veil

When the bride leaves her house she wears a veil to let other men know that she is spoken for; no touchy! She is off limits because she has been bought with a price. She is set apart and will resist any other offers as she waits for her true love. The veil would be comparable to our engagement ring. It's a sign of the covenant.

Her Job

The Shulammite girl prepares for her wedding by making things for the house: blankets, potholders, and crafts that will end up at a yard sale (just kidding). Her neighbors will have bridal showers for her as she prepares to put the personal touches on their home.

During this time away from her groom she is to mend broken relationships with friends and family members. The Hebrew men were no dummies. They didn't want a woman coming into the marriage relationship with a lot of baggage (anger, bitterness, jealousy); it's also a time for her is to show gratitude to her family for raising her.

Her most important job, however, is to find out all she can about the groom and his family. What are his favorite foods? Does he like red or pink toenail polish; dry-cleaned or laundered shirts? Is he allergic to anything? What does he love to do in his spare time? Boy, if only I had known this going into my marriage I could have saved myself a lot of grief. I was working myself to death trying to please my man, only to realize that Mexican food fixes everything. So I learned how to make green chili, salsa, and refried beans!

Our job while we wait for our groom is clear and simple. We are to find out all we can about Christ, fix broken relationships, and love one another.

Prepared at all Times

The Shulammite girl's second most important job is to be prepared for his return at all times. She never knows when he may be coming for her. Her dress is pressed, makeup bag is prepared, and her lingerie is neatly packed. Her life is to be in order because she never knows when her last day at home will be.

Bridesmaids

Under the Jewish tradition the bride is to pick unmarried virgins to be her bridesmaids. They attend to the bride and are to have oil in their lamps at all times. Their job is to provide light for the bride, as the groom usually comes at night or in the wee hours of the morning. Imagine what she will look like if she has to dress and put on her makeup in the dark. The second reason to have oil in their lamps is to light the path back to the bridal chamber.

Oil represents the Holy Spirit in our lives. We are to ask and be filled with It, we are to be a light unto the world. Those without it don't look so hot and tend to stumble in the dark.

Groomsmen

When the time comes for Solomon to get his bride, he wants to surprise her but he also needs to give her a warning so she can be ready to go with him, so he sends his groomsmen ahead of him. They run in front and shout and blow a shofar (ram's horn) to let the bride know her bridegroom is coming. The whole town is filled with excitement as Solomon makes a grand entry into the town. He wants to make sure everyone notices that there is going to a wedding.

During the commotion Solomon goes into the bride's house and swoops her up into his arms. He steals his bride.

Jesus tells us that "The Lord Himself will descend from heaven with a shout, with the voice of the archangel and with the trumpet of God, and the dead in Christ will rise first. Then we who are alive and remain will be caught up together with them in the cloud to meet the Lord in the air, and so we shall always be with the Lord" (I Thessalonians 4:16).

I think the town will notice that there is going to be a wedding when angels shout, trumpets blow, and dead people fly by their heads. I'm sure it's going to leave a lasting impression (I Thessalonians 4:16).

Seven Days in the Bridal Chamber (*Huppah*):

After the town is all stirred up, excited, and bewildered, the wedding party returns to the house of the bridegroom's father. In this case, Solomon takes her to the palace. The couple goes into the wedding chamber (*huppah*) for a seven-day honeymoon. While in the chamber Solomon honors the last part of the *ketubah*. He gives her pleasure, if you know what I mean!

Stained Sheets

The young couple has intercourse; the bride's hymen is broken, and blood on the sheets shows if she is a true virgin. The second phase of the wedding is complete; the blood covenant of marriage has now been sealed. The two are one.

The groom's best friend stands outside the door, waiting for the groom to tell him the marriage has be consummated. At the appropriate moment, Solomon takes the honeymoon sheet, stained with blood, and gives it to his best friend. This special friend presents the bloodstained sheet to those gathered to celebrate. The party begins; the couple has become one. Friends and family celebrate for seven days until the newlyweds emerge from their bridal chamber.

"What if the bride isn't a virgin?" you ask.

Jewish weddings usually took place on Wednesdays because the courts were in session on Thursdays. Therefore, if a bride wasn't pure, the groom had a few options. He could get a divorce called "a get" and never see her again or he could have her stoned or killed.

I would like to suggest something else to you. I think if the groom really loves his bride he will pierce himself and put his blood on the sheets so that he can present her to his father and friends as pure. I believe his love for her will cause him to protect her from humiliation.

Wedding Feast

When the new couple makes their appearance, the guests clap and cheer and congratulate them. There is singing and dancing, followed by a joyous feast called the marriage supper, which is given to honor of the new husband and wife.

The new couple leaves their fathers' and mothers' and cleaves to each other, thus beginning their new life.

Now that we understand the wedding customs, let's get back to the relationship of the Shulammite girl and Solomon.

After the Betrothal

"Until the cool of the day when the shadows flee away, turn, my beloved, and be like a gazelle or a young stag on the mountains of Bether" (Song of Solomon 2:17).

Every since their betrothal, daydreaming about Solomon has become the Shulammite girl's favorite pastime. She dreams about spending every night with her love. She dreams of him on her breasts (mountains of Bether) all night long; but until their wedding day she must wait.

"On my bed night after night I sought him whom my soul loves; I sought him but did not find him" (Song of Solomon 3:1). After months of waiting our Shulammite girl tosses and turns in her bed night after night and wonders, "will this be the night that my love returns for me?" In the middle of the night fear grips her, "what if my love doesn't come back for me? Does he really love me? What if his promises aren't true? I am nothing without him." She fears his proposal is too good to be true.

Over and over in her head she recites the *ketubah* that Solomon gave her. She knows it contained his obligations: protection, provision, and pleasure. Legally they are married but she feels unsure while they are apart. She begins to focus on all the things that could go wrong before the second phase of the wedding. What she is really struggling with is trusting in the promises of her groom.

Isn't that the way it is for us? In the middle of the night, the kiss of fear grips our souls. We wake up and worry about school, friends, family situations, money, jobs, and everything else under the sun because we either don't know what Christ has promised us in our *ketubah* or we don't have the faith to believe it.

This scared feeling is more than the Shulammite girl can bear. In the wee hours of the morning she finds herself dressed and on her way searching for answers. "I must arise now and go about the city; in the streets and in the squares I must seek him whom my soul loves" (Song of Solomon 3:2). At first she can't find Solomon but when she inquires of the watchmen, who see everything, they point her in the direction of Solomon (Song of Solomon 3:3-4).

Girls we are to do the same. We are to "seek Him whom our soul loves." Jesus tells us, "But seek first the kingdom and His righteousness and all these things shall be added unto you" (Matthew 6:33). Get up early in the morning and spend time reading your *ketubah* (Bible), seeking your groom. I can just hear some of you saying, "I read but none of it makes sense to me." You may need to inquire of the watchmen (mature Christians) to help you find Him and to help you understand the scriptures.

May I be that watchman to you for a brief moment and help you understand your covenant (*ketubah*)?

Imagine yourself as the King of Kings pulls up to your doorway on His magnificent white horse followed by His legions of angels. He enters into your filthy sin—infested house. His love fills the room as He unrolls His scroll and presents to you His *ketubah*. He looks at your mother and says, "I would like to offer your daughter a new covenant."

Christ offers you a new *ketubah*. "New" in the Greek is *kahee-nos* and means "freshness, regenerate." The word "New" in the Hebrew is from the root word *khaw-dash* it means, "to rebuild, renew, and repair." Jesus is saying, "I came to rebuild, renew, repair Abraham's everlasting covenant" (Genesis. 17:7).

Jesus proceeds with His proposal. "I've come to offer provision. All the Kingdom's physical and spiritual wealth I offer to your daughter. Now as for her protection, I offer your daughter legions of angels" (Hebrews 1:14).

"And yes, Mrs. *(fill in your last name)*, I would like to be intimate with your daughter. I want to pour my Spirit into hers so that she will have great power. I want to write My laws on her heart so that she will know My will and put My laws into her mind so that she will know how to speak and act" (Hebrews 8:10).

"But that's not all. There is more to My *ketubah*," states Jesus. "I will take all of her grief and bear her sorrows. I will be pierced for her sins. Your daughter will never be guilty again; I will take her guilt away. I love your daughter so much that I'm going to be punished so that she will have well being. Oh yeah, there's one more thing: I'm going to take a beating that would kill most men, because I want your daughter to be healed" (Isaiah 53).

Here's My *moha*r . . . My life.

Jesus is saying to you, "I want your worries, your problems, your health issues, your financial issues, and your friendship issues to go away. Will you accept my offer or reject it?"

As you bring that communion cup to your lips remember that you said "yes" and the first part of the wedding has taken place. You now have worth, protection, provision, an everlasting love.

As the Shulammite girl searches, she finds Solomon and says, "Scarcely had I left them (the watchmen) when I found him whom my soul loves; I held on to him and would not let him go until I had brought him to my mother's house and into the room of her who conceived me" (Song of Solomon 3:4). What she is saying to us is once she knew her covenant, once she knew it was true she felt so safe, so secure, as if she were under the covers of her mother's bed. Her mother's room is a picture of safety.

Have you ever been scared in the middle of the night? As little girls, my sisters and I shared a bedroom in our basement. I would wake up in the middle of the night scared to death. I knew that if I could just be brave enough to run upstairs and crawl into my parents' bed, I would be safe. The moment I could snuggle between them and pull the covers up under my chin, I would sleep like a baby knowing that nothing would be able to get me. My dad was strong and my protector and my mom comforted me. I was safe in my parents' bed.

Girls, once we get to know our groom and His covenant (*ketubah*), we will be like a little kid, so safe, so secure under her parent's covers.

I met a beautiful, single young woman at a speaker's conference who had figured His *ketubah* out for her. She was different than all of the other women there. She had a bounce to her step, a glow on her face and a confidence that was demonstrated by her posture.

I asked this woman, "Where does all of your confidence come from?"

She replied, "I know what Jesus did on the cross for me." She continued, "As a young successful businesswoman I use to go in and have my nails done. The nail tech I went to gave me flat warts. They were all over my hands. The next thing I knew they had spread to my face. I was a mess. My doctor told me that the only way to get rid of them was to burn them off chemically, so I proceeded with the treatment. A few days later my face became as large as a basketball. Upon returning to the doctors, they informed me that I needed to be put on a seven-day pack of steroids. My face returned to normal but something was wrong with me as I began to lose sleep. Night after night, I would go to bed and an electric-like shock would go down my legs. After years of this, I began to see doctors from all over the country. I was even checked into a mental hospital at one point. I feared the night. Many nights my sister would hold me and I would cry in her arms. I didn't want to live anymore and twice I tried to commit suicide. Each time my sister saved my life."

"My spiritual mentor kept telling me, 'when are you going to stop trusting in man for your healing and start trusting in God?' I knew what she was saying but I just couldn't seem to totally trust God."

"After five years of being a zombie, I remember sitting at my computer desk and a Bible verse, Ephesians 3:16-19, began to tick across the bottom of the screen, 'that He would grant you, according to the riches of His glory, to be strengthened with power through His Spirit in the inner man, so that Christ may dwell in your hearts through faith; and that you, being rooted and grounded in love, may be able to comprehend with all the saints what is the breadth and length and height and depth, and to know the love of Christ which surpasses knowledge, that you may be filled up to all the fullness of God.' I realized that I had been limiting God and all that He had for me. I realized that He had taken care of everything on the cross. I raised my hands and said, Thank you Jesus for taking care of that!"

"I went home and flushed all the sleeping pills down the toilet and realized that Jesus was my healer. I lay on my bed that first night and didn't sleep a wink, but I believed that His words were true. I kept thanking Jesus for 'taking care of that.' The next day at work I raised my hands anytime fear or doubt crossed my mind and said, 'Thank you, Jesus, for taking care of that!"

"On the second night, I went to bed and slept like a baby all through the night for the first time in five years and I've been sleeping every since. 'Thank you Jesus for taking care of that!'"

This young woman knows her *ketubah*. She now sleeps like a child safely tucked under the covers of her parents.

Oh, sweet girl, get to know Him, seek His face, because when you find "Him, whom your soul loves," you will be so safe, so secure, so protected under the *ketubah* that He has given to you. Don't put a limit on what He wants to pour out to you. Just receive it and snuggle underneath its warm blanket.

Kingdom Challenge:

I challenge you to time yourself and see how long it takes you to get ready in the morning. However long it takes you to get ready, I want you to get up that much earlier and spend uninterrupted time with God, reading, praying, memorizing scripture, or studying. For example, if it takes you fifteen minutes to get ready, set your alarm fifteen minutes earlier and have a quiet time with God.

Today's One-liner:... The Word Is My *Ketubah*
Clue For Living "Happily Ever After": .... Matthew 6:33

> *"But seek first His kingdom and His righteousness, and all these thing will be added to you."*

Kiss of Love:...Know *Ketubah*
Kiss of Betrayal:... No *Ketubah*

Chapter Six

The Wedding

"I have come into my garden, my sister, my bride;
I have gathered my myrrh along with my balsam.
I have eaten my honeycomb and my honey;
I have drunk my wine and my milk.
Drink and imbibe deeply, O lovers."
Song of Solomon 5:1

It was the day our daughter, Jolene, had dreamed of her whole life. She was about to marry to her prince, Jeffrey. They'd planned a simple yet elegant wedding in our backyard.

Our family gathered around the breakfast table early in the morning. We prayed together, asked God to bless the day, and shed a few tears, knowing that this would be the last time it would just be the six of us. We were about to be joined to another tribe.

The sun came up over the Grand Mesa and dried the morning dew. People scurried around the house, adding the final wedding touches.

Beautiful purple, white, and raspberry-colored petunias, tangerine daisies, white geraniums, and lush green vines flowed over the large pots that were delivered by the local nursery. Wreaths of matching flowers were placed at the base of Old World lanterns that illuminated the stone columns around our courtyard. Caterers set up tables and decorated buffet lines while the deejay set up his speakers and amps.

White chairs stood in perfect symmetry in our backyard overlooking our pond and pastures where the horses grazed and ducks had congregated for such an occasion as this.

On the south side of the yard was a surreal scene—wreaths holding oil lanterns floated on a calm, glassy pool. The light gave an ambience to the greenery and flowers that surrounded them.

At one end of the pool a white cabaña was draped with netting. The netting was softly pulled back with long flowing ribbons to form a doorway. Inside the cabaña a delightful array of fresh fruit, cheese and crackers were laid out. This area would provide the perfect place to serve our guests hor d'oeuvres.

The majestic red rocks of the Colorado National Monument provided the backdrop for the setting. *Could anything be prettier?* I thought.

As the sun gave way to dusk, the guests would venture through the ornate Iron Gate that connected two large stone columns covered with vines. Their eyes would be greeted with the romance of soft candle light, rose petals, linens, and buffet tables that would please any king.

A fairytale wedding was about to take place.

The bridesmaids started showing up around 11:00 a.m. There was much to do. A make-up artist tweezed eyebrows, fixed dark circles under tired eyes, and transformed each girl into a beauty.

The hairstylist went to work ratting, combing, and spraying, until each young woman had the perfect hairdo. They were drop-dead gorgeous.

Jolene was taking it all in. It would be her last day as a single woman. She reminisced with her friends and sisters about old times as they all went through the beautification together.

Jeffrey and his groomsmen prepared for the ceremony at the opposite end of the house.

As the time drew near, the florist handed out bouquets, flower baskets, and boutonnières. Grandparents showed up and received instructions on where to be for pictures. The valet attendants stood waiting for their first cars to park. The house buzzed with excitement and the photographers captured each moment.

As the clock stuck 6:00 p.m., the moment we had all waited for came.

Jeff and his groomsmen entered the backyard to take their places in front of the congregation. T.J., a six-foot-eight-inch pastor took his place underneath the arbor of flowers. The groom's parents then walked down the aisle that separated the two families, preceded by the bride's mother.

One by one, the beautiful young bridesmaids wafted down the aisle as if they were floating on air. They stood before the congregation on the bride's side.

Laughter and smiles erupted as the little ring bearer entered wearing a suit that seemed to have swallowed him up. The flower girl stole the show as she strategically placed each rose petal.

At a moment's notice, the music changed. Four loud chords let the guests know that something exciting was about to happen. I stood and every guest followed my cue and turned toward the center of the aisle.

We gasped at the grandeur that our eyes were beholding. At the back entryway, a beautiful young bride stood next to her father, the man who had provided, protected, and loved her with all of his heart since her birth. Jolene wrapped her arm around her dad's and Jay drew her close to him as if to say, "I don't want to let you go."

As the beautiful bride made her way down the aisle a tear trickled down the cheek of the groom. Her beauty, their love, and the splendor of the moment were almost more than any of us could bear.

T.J. asked, "Who gives this bride to this man?"

"Her mother and I," my husband said in a low voice choked with emotion. He removed Jolene's hand from his arm and united her with Jeffrey.

The couple stood before the crowd and recited their *ketubah*.

Jolene's eyes sparkled beneath her veil as she said, "I, Jolene, take you, Jeffrey, to be my wedded husband; and I promise, before God and these witnesses, to be your loving and faithful wife, in plenty and in want, in joy and in sorrow, in sickness and in health, as long as we both shall live."

Jeffrey gazed into her eyes as he said the same vows. Jeffrey then took the ring from his best man and slid in onto Jolene's slender finger. "I give you this ring in token of the covenant made today between us; in the name of the Father, and of the Son, and of the Holy Spirit."

Jolene's maid of honor passed her Jeffrey's ring. She held his hand as she eased it over his knuckle. "I give you this ring in token of the covenant made today between us; in the name of the Father, and of the Son, and of the Holy Spirit."

The preacher solemnly announced, "I now pronounce them man and wife."

Jeffrey lifted the veil that separated him from his bride. He pulled her toward him and gave her the kiss of *chashaq*; a deep, gentle, I-love-you kiss; a kiss where no words need to be spoken.

My husband said, as only a man can, "Let the relationship begin!" It was time to enjoy the second stage of the marriage: consummation. The newlyweds would venture away from their fathers and mothers and into their promised land where "the two shall become one" (Genesis 2:24).

The Music Changes

In Solomon's land the markets are full of people buying and selling. Goats are led down from Gilead to be slaughtered. The Feast of Tabernacle is quickly approaching and Jews are coming to Jerusalem from all parts of the world to celebrate the holiday. There's an excitement in the air; then, in a twinkling of an eye, the music changes.

"What is this coming up from the wilderness like columns of smoke, perfumed with myrrh and frankincense, and with all scented powders of the merchants?" (Song of Solomon 3:6)

I envision a thick, dark, dust evaporates from the desert's floor, as the sound of thundering horses grows near. Fear grips the city. "Warriors from a distant land are coming to attack!" scream the watchmen.

People drop whatever they have in their hands and run for their lives. Suddenly fear turns to jubilation when the familiar sound of the king's shofar is heard. The memorable sound of the ram's horn signals that a wedding is about to take place, not a war.

Oh, sweet girls, our God is such a romantic because this is exactly how He presented Himself to His bride, the Israelites thousands of years ago. He led her through the desert by a pillar of cloud by day and a pillar of fire by night (Exodus 13-21). People everywhere took notice as God brought her into the promise land (*huppah*).

We can rest assured that the day our Lord comes back for us will be no less thrilling. He's giving us a preview to the sequel that is to come and, unlike most movie sequels; this one is going to be better than the first.

Wake Up

"Wake up, wake up," someone calls and pounds on the Shulammite girl's door.

"It's Solomon and his entourage!" shouts a bridesmaid.

Every lantern in the house is lit while the bride begins to prepare for the big moment. Her bridesmaids attend to her nervously. They help her slip into her dress and gather her things.

Perched high upon his purple sedan chair, Solomon rides into town in a grand fashion. He is surrounded by the mighty men of Israel, wielders of the sword, and experts in war.

The mighty men of Israel have one job—to protect the king and his interests. Today the king's only interest is to marry the beautiful young Shulammite girl. The mighty men of Israel take full command with their swords; no enemy dare go near them or he will lose his head. Under their careful eye nothing will be able to stop this wedding.

This scene is a picture for us. We are to wield our sword (use the Word of God with full command) along with the rest of our armor so that we protect our hearts and minds from the enemy's attacks (Ephesians 6:10-12).

Our enemy isn't other people. It's a spiritual enemy and as I've said before, Satan's favorite battlefield is our minds. We are God's interest and while He has given us tools to use to defend ourselves, He has also given us extra help in the form of mighty Angels to guard and protect us so that nothing can stop our wedding to Him (Hebrews 1:14).

As the sedan chair is lowered to the ground, Solomon steps down, dressed in the royal attire. Upon his head he wears a wedding crown or wreath, not his usual crown of authority. He will enter into the bride's home and swoop her up in his arms, place her in the sedan chair, and the two of them will be carried to the bridal chamber, where they will spend the next seven days.

I want to warn you, we are about to enter another "no-spin zone:" the bridal chamber. What you are about to see with your imagination is passionate, hot stuff, but only if you understand it.

A few months ago our daughter, Jordan, jumped in the back seat of our Yukon after church. She said, "Our pastor told us that if we wanted to read something that really brings on the heat, we should read Song of Solomon chapter four."

She grabbed my Bible and started to read, "'How beautiful you are, my darling, how beautiful you are!' Okay, that's not so bad," she said with a sigh. "'Your eyes are like doves behind your veil; your hair like a flock of goats that have descended from Mount Gilead? Your teeth . . .'" (Song of Solomon 4:1) she read as her voice trailed off. "This is the stupidest thing I've ever heard. Where's the heat?" She shrugged her shoulders.

I laughed and told Jordan, "If you understand the customs and history you will see that this is one of the most beautiful love stories of all time."

Even though we dream about our wedding and honeymoon our whole lives, the unknown can be scary. Solomon knows this about his bride so he doesn't just rush right into the bridal chamber and say, "Down . . . set . . . hut! hut!" And then take her to the ground like a football player making his first big tackle.

Solomon is patient and loving, not to mention smart. He knows something about a woman that is very important. He knows that sex for a woman starts in her mind.

Solomon begins with her mind. He wants her to see her beauty, her worth as he sees it. He wants her to be comfortable with her own body. He knows that if she is proud of her body she will not be afraid to show it to him. And he wants to see her in full form (Song of Solomon 2:14).

With words Solomon slowly paints a portrait of her. He begins to verbally describe seven of her body parts. Starting with her head, he works his way down to her breasts. He is meticulous with meanings and symbols as the number seven in Hebrew means perfect, and the word bride means to complete. Solomon wants her to see that without her he is not whole.

Solomon stands before his bride. With his hands holding her cheeks, he whispers, "How beautiful you are, my darling, how beautiful you are! Your eyes are like doves behind your veil" (Song of Solomon 4:1). He reminds her how much he appreciates that she only has eyes for him, and how loved he feels when he looks into her gentle spirit.

"Your hair is like a flock of goats that have descended from Mount Gilead" (Song of Solomon 4:1). Most of us would knock Solomon up side of the head with our purse if he said this to us, but she is getting a different picture. Mount Gilead was in the Transjordan river valley right outside the promise land. It was a beautiful place; in fact, two and one half tribes decided to go back there after the Israelites conquered the promised land. Goats were a sign of wealth and flocks looked like beautiful wavy hair as they descended down the mountain. Solomon is telling her that she prospers him. She is not a ball and chain she is an asset.

"Your teeth are like a flock of newly shorn ewes which have come up from their washing, all of which bear twins" (Song of Solomon 4:2). I imagine Solomon says with a sigh of relief. His bride isn't toothless. Her teeth are white, straight, and none are missing. This could be a good argument for braces. I don't know about you, but I get the giggles when I think about Solomon lifting her veil and finding a woman with her front teeth missing. Can't you just see him saying, "Thank you, Lord, she has all her teeth!"

Now on the serious side, Solomon is not only telling her how beautiful her smile is he's telling her something spiritually deep. In those days they didn't have baby food grinders. It would be up to the mother to chew up the food for her babies and then feed it to them. It's a metaphor to her and us that as godly women we are to take the word of God and chew it up so that we can feed it to our children. He's telling her that she is going to be an excellent mother.

He continues, "Your lips are like a scarlet thread, and your mouth is lovely" (Song of Solomon 4:3). Red lips were a sign of good health and beauty. A thin thread meant that she chose her words carefully, eager to praise and not to tear people down with her lips.

"Your temples are like a slice of a pomegranate behind your veil" (Song of Solomon 4:3). Solomon's patience and self-control are to be commended, as He hasn't even taken her veil off yet. Pomegranates describe modesty and humility. They also represent love. She is full of love, and she's blushing because Solomon has just compared her to Mother Earth.

Solomon draws her near, lifting her veil so that he may touch her lips ever so softly with his. His head tilts toward her as he kisses her with the kiss of *chashaq*; the kiss where no words need to be spoken. The kiss that says I will protect you, provide for you, and I am committed to you. The same kiss Phillip gave Sleeping Beauty, the deep gentle, I-love-you, passionate, yet soft kiss. It's time to let the relationship begin.

His hands slide down from her head to her neck. "Your neck is like the tower of David, built with rows of stones on which are hung a thousand shields, all the round shields of the mighty men" (Song of Solomon 4:4). What a compliment for her to even be in the same category as fighting warriors.

The tower of David was a memorial to soldiers who had lost their lives fighting for their promised land. The soldiers' shields would be hung on the rows of stones and displayed for all to see. They served as an encouragement to young soldiers and reminded them that their land was worth fighting for.

The Tower of David was also part of the city wall. It guarded the western entrance to Jerusalem. The tower was built at this location because the entrance was considered the weak link in the city's defense. The tower would guard the promise land from enemies.

Are you starting to see what I'm seeing? Up until this point the Shulammite girl is described as the Transjordan river valley, which is right outside the promise land. It's beautiful, but it's not the promise land.

Men know that there is something better than looking at your beautiful face. They too have heard about or experienced the promise land. They want to go in (have sex) and it takes a guarded, strong tower and the faith of a fighting warrior to keep them out.

The Shulammite girl has hung her shield around her neck (faith) and guarded her city. She has kept men out of the land that is promised to her husband. Sexually, she is pure, and this is an encouragement for others to know that it is possible to stay a virgin until marriage.

Slowly Solomon begins to undress his bride. His eyes gaze upon her breasts. "Your two breasts are like two fawns, twins of a gazelle, which feed among the lilies" (Song of Solomon 4:5). He compares her breast to two fawns; fawns are babies, they are little. There is absolutely nothing wrong with small breasts. In fact, he thinks they're wonderful and would like to enjoy them.

The warrior in Solomon wanted to capture these little creatures, taste them, touch them, and be satisfied by them. He knows not to rush upon gazelles while eating. He's going to have to be methodical and move slowly and carefully so he won't scare them away if he wants to enjoy them at his banqueting table (I Kings 4:23).

The woman's breasts are a very sensitive organ; when touched it can either simulate her sexually or really turn her off. The way it is approached is important and so is the state of her mind. God tells us that He created them to bring our husband pleasure and us. "Let your fountain be blessed, and rejoice in the wife of your youth. As a loving hind and a graceful doe, let her breast satisfy you at all times, be exhilarated always with her love" (Proverbs 5:18-19).

"Until the cool of the day when the shadows flee away, I will go my way to the mountain of myrrh and to the hill of frankincense" (Song of Solomon 4:6). Solomon tells his new bride that he longs to be on her breast all night long. But why would he call them the mountain of myrrh (bitterness) and hill of frankincense (sweet)?

Some scholars believe that the two breasts represent the two tablets that the Ten Commandments were written on. Others say they represent the two sacraments (the bread and wine) of the New Covenant.

May I suggest to you another thought? I believe the breasts represent Mt. Gerizim (blessings) and Mt. Ebal (curses). These were the two mountains that the Israelites passed through before entering the promise land.

Finally, the Promise Land

After forty years of wandering, the Israelites finally stood on the edge of the wilderness, looking into the promise land. What a sight! There was flowing water, grapes, pomegranates, figs, and lush green hillsides with goats feeding on them. It was a land flowing with milk and honey (Numbers 14:8).

Before they entered into the promise land, God stopped the Israelites at the base of two mountains: Mt. Ebal and Mt. Gerizim. Mt. Ebal represented curses and Mt. Gerizim represented blessings (Deuteronomy 11:29). The only thing that separated these two mountains was a valley or a cleavage.

BiblePlaces.com

Mt. Ebal and Mt. Gerizum

As you will see in Deuteronomy 27:13-26 and 28:1-11, before the Israelites could enter the promise land, God told them to send six men to stand on top of Mt. Ebal to represent half of the twelve tribes. On top of Mt. Gerizim six more men stood to represent the other tribes. The Levites (priests) stood in the cleavage of the rock with the Ark of the Covenant. The tribes on Mt. Ebal yelled out all of the curses that would come upon the Israelites if they didn't keep God's ways. After each curse the people shouted "Amen," which meant that they agreed.

"Cursed is the Man who makes an idol!" shouted the tribe.

"Amen!" replied the people!

"Cursed is the man who dishonors his father or mother."

"Amen!"

"Cursed is he who deals falsely with his neighbor."

"Amen!"

"Cursed is he who misleads a blind person."

"Amen!"

"Cursed is he who lies."

"Amen!"

"Cursed is he who commits adultery, fornication or incest"

"Amen!"

The Israelites jumped up and down, high-fiving each other, determined not to live their lives with curses. They had dwelt in the desert a long time, dreaming about entering into the promise land, and they didn't want to blow it now.

A silence fell over the crowd as the blessings were shouted from Mt. Gerizim.

"Now it shall be if you will diligently obey the Lord your God, being careful to do all His commandments which I command you today the Lord your God will set you high above all the nations of the earth."

"Blessings shall come upon you and overtake you if you will obey the Lord your God." In other words, He'll bless your socks off.

"Blessed shall you be in the city and blessed shall you be in the country."

"Blessed shall be the offspring of your body and the produce of your ground and the offspring of your beasts, the increase of your heard and the young of your flock."

"Blessed shall be your basket and your kneading bowl."

"Blessed shall you be when you come in and blessed shall you be when you go out."

"The Lord will cause your enemies who rise up against you to be defeated before you."

"The Lord will command the blessing upon you in your barns and in all that you put your hand to and He will bless you in the land which the Lord your God gives you."

"The Lord will establish you as a holy people to Himself as He swore to you if you will keep the commandment of the Lord your God, and walk in His ways."

And finally the tribe shouted, "The Lord will make you abound in prosperity in the offspring of your body and in offspring of your beast and in the produce of your ground in the land which the Lord swore to your fathers to give you."

I don't know about you but I want to shout, "Show me your ways!"

As the people walked through the cleavage of the two mountains, they were reminded to choose God's ways and to live their lives with blessings in their new promised land. It was a reminder of their covenant.

Solomon is at the cleavage of his sexual promised land. He has a choice to make. Will he keep his covenant with his bride? Will her always love her, protect her, provide for her, and be faithful to her, which will bring blessings to his family? Or will he choose not to love her, cheat on her when things get rough, and bail on her if finances get tight, bringing curses to his family?

The breasts remind Solomon that if the married couple keep their vows to one another and stay faithful to one another they are going to have the blessings of an amazing marriage, not to mention sex life.

As Solomon passes through the cleavage of the breasts, his heart beats faster and faster. He kisses her and undresses her while he whispers to her, "Your lips, my bride, drip honey; honey and milk are under your tongue" (Song of Solomon 4:11).

He tastes honey and milk under her tongue. We call this French kissing, but God calls it the kiss of *nasaq,* the kiss of passion, fire, and burning. In the middle of passion, they can't get close enough to each other; their bodies are burning with desire for one another and physically they begin to change.

"You are altogether beautiful, my darling. And there is no blemish in you" (Song of Solomon 4:7). He has fully undressed her and he loves everything about her, the way she smells, the taste of her lips, and the curves of her soft body. "A garden locked is my sister, my bride, a rock garden locked, a spring sealed up" (Song of Solomon 4:12). Solomon once again compliments her that she is a virgin and he wants to come into her garden.

The Shulammite bride has waited a long time for this moment. "Awake, O north wind, and come, wind of the south, make my garden breathe out fragrance, let its spices be wafted abroad. May my beloved come into his garden and eat its choice fruits!" she says (Song of Solomon 4:16). She is excited and ready for the sexual part of their relationship to begin. She calls her body his garden and she wants him to enjoy it.

Girls, I assure you that what these two are doing in the bridal chamber is a beautiful thing. Her body no longer belongs to her. It belongs to Solomon. His body no longer belongs to him. It belongs to his bride (1 Corinthians 7:3-5). They both desire to please one another.

Solomon doesn't hesitate but eagerly goes into the promised land of sex. He gathers the best spices, eats the honey and drinks his wine and milk. It is all and more than God has promised.

When the consummation is complete, God says to the couple, "Eat, friends; drink and imbibe deeply, soak it in like a sponge, O lovers" (Song of Solomon 5:1). Let the celebration begin; the two are now one!

Solomon joyfully takes the bloodstained sheet to his best man. The best man presents the sheet to the wedding party. Solomon's father, if still living would have been proud that his son kept her pure. Then with great joy he would have alerted the guests to come and share in the wedding feast.

I know that there are some of you reading this right now who may be saddened by this scene because you have had sex in the past. You may think that you've ruined your chance to have a promised-land experience on your honeymoon night. I want to tell you that that is a kiss of betrayal. You can rebuild the wall and strong tower and redefine the promise land. God says that He can and will make all things new (2 Corinthians 5:17). But you are going to have to want to rebuild the tower, and only you can desire to put up the security system.

Girls ask me all the time, "how far is too far when you're dating someone?" Call me a fuddy-duddy but I believe that the scripture is very clear. When Solomon described her head it was the Transjordan river valley; everything outside the promise land. The neck is the wall that protects the city. Your breasts are the entrance to the Promised Land. Keep guys hands out of your blouses and out of your pants! I know that your jaws are probably dropping right now, but please listen. I wish someone had shared with me that my body is a promised land. God is giving us a picture. The neck is the wall; it's the strong tower where you watch for the enemy. You don't want enemies in your promised land. No one passes through the cleavage of the breast except the one whom you are in covenant with. He has presented to you a *ketubah* and paid the price (*mohar*).

If you want to rebuild the promise land, it is totally possible. But it is going take diet, discipline, and exercise.

Rebuilding the Promised Land

Keep the junk food out of your mind. Stop reading all the magazines that tell you how you are to act and look. Get rid of friends that drag you down. Get your self-image from what God says about you. And God says you are fearfully and wonderfully made (Psalms 139:14).

Discipline

Discipline yourself to spend time reading the Word of God, seeking your Prince Jesus; know what truth is. Again I encourage you to spend the same amount of time you take getting ready each day with God in the word. Also, get into a good Bible study.

Exercise

The best exercise for redefining the body is weight lifting. I'm standing up cheering for you while I type this because I want to become your spiritual trainer and coach. Muscles get bigger because pressure is applied and resisted too. The more we resist pressure, the more defined we are going to be.

When you decide to start over with sexual purity you may hear something like this: "You did it with John, why not me?" Satan has just put the bench press bar in your hands. He's applying pressure to your chest; it's heavy. You might be tempted to give in to it. Your week mind might rationalize: "What's the use to try and stay pure? I've blown it; I'm never going to have a promise land experience."

It's time to lift the bar off of your chest with authority. Read 2 Corinthians 5:17, and start pumping it into your mind, and then start saying it: "Therefore if anyone is in Christ, he is a new creature; the old things have passed away; behold, new things have come." The more you pump your mind with this weight, the stronger it's going to get. You will start seeing yourself in a new way, not as old friends have labeled you. You will be able to respond with boldness to any young man, "I'm not the same person I once was!" You will begin to lift the bar off of your chest as if it weighed nothing.

When the nasty comments come at you: "She's easy. She's slept with everyone! Adulterous woman!" Pump another spiritual weight into your brain, like the Bible story of Jesus defending the woman caught in adultery. He said to her accusers, "He who is without sin among you? Let him be the first to throw a stone at her." Then He said to the woman, "Woman, where are they? Did no one condemn you?"

She said, "No one, Lord."

Jesus said, "I do not condemn you, either. Go. From now on sin no more" (John 83-11).

It's easy to recover your reputation when you realize that no one is without sin. Hold your head up and sin no more. Your accusers are gone.

When you first start to diet, people don't take you seriously. But when they start seeing the results of someone who is committed, there is a new respect. Keep up your diet, discipline, and exercise so that on your wedding night you will have great confidence in your new, defined body.[3] You will want to share it with

---

3 Weight-lifting terminology from son-in-law Charlie Beckman (weight trainer)

your groom and enjoy the words, "You are altogether beautiful, my darling. And there is no blemish in you" (Song of Solomon 4:7). What joy when God says to you, "Eat, friends; drink and imbibe deeply, O lovers" (Song of Solomon 5:1).

The Music Will Change

One day you'll be living life as usual and the music will change. You will hear the loud trumpet. Scripture tells us that, just like the Jewish groom comes for his bride, Jesus is coming for us.

Jesus will descend from heaven, with a shout, with the voice of the archangel, and with the trumpet of God (*shofar*). The dead in Christ will rise first. Then we who are alive and remain will be caught up together with them in the clouds to meet the Lord in the air, and so we shall always be with the Lord (I Thessalonians 4:16-18).

We will be safe in the bridal chamber. But on earth there is going to be great destruction. This is the beginning of the great tribulation. Once it starts it will last for seven years. After seven years of tribulation, Jesus will bring us (his bride) back to earth dressed in fine linen, white and clean; for the fine linen is the righteous acts of the saints (Revelations 19:7-9).

I believe Revelation 19:11-13 paints us a picture of our groom coming out of the bridal chamber, the heavens will open and Christ will be on a white horse. He will be called Faithful and True. His eyes will be a flame of fire, and on His head are many crowns. He will not be carrying a white sheet stained with our blood. He is clothed in a robe dipped in blood. I believe He knew we weren't pure but He loved us so much that He covered us. He pierced His own hands and put His blood on the sheet. There will be no humiliation, no divorce, no stoning, only rejoicing as we are presented as beautiful, young virgins before His father and the wedding party.

Oh, to hear the words of His Father: "Eat, friends; drink and imbibe deeply, O lovers" (Song of Solomon 5:1). Let the celebration begin!

Kingdom Challenge:

Write a letter to your future husband. Tell him how you've been praying for him. Give him a vision of what you want your honeymoon night to be like. Share with him if you desire to protect the promise land or if you've failed and want to rebuild your strong tower. Then seal the letter and share it with him on your wedding day.

Today's One-liner:..Jesus, My Groom
Clue for living "Happily Ever After":.............................. 1 Corinthians 7:3-5

> *"The wife doesn't have authority over her own body, but the husband does, and likewise also the husband does not have authority over his own body, but the wife does. Stop depriving one another."*

Kiss of Love:.. There Is No Blemish in You
Kiss of Betrayal:... Blemished

Chapter Seven

"Happily Ever After"

"See, I have set before you today life and prosperity, and death and adversity."
Deuteronomy 30:15

What a journey we've been on. We've watched as an insignificant peasant girl dreamed of kissing Prince Solomon. He wasn't just any prince; he was a man who wore great-smelling cologne, had a great name, and was related to the Prince of Peace.

Through his kind remarks, self-control, faithfulness, patience and gentleness Solomon kissed the Shulammite girl with the kiss of *phileo* (friendship). It wasn't long before Solomon's friendship drew the Shulammite girl to the palace, where she learned the protocol of the kingdom, became a beautiful princess, and received the king's favor, not to mention his love.

It was a romantic time as they watched the stars at night and ran together during the day. Everyone in town could see that his banner over her was love.

After spending time together, respecting one another, complimenting each other, and playing hours of Monopoly, Solomon presented to her a *ketubah*. "Arise, my darling my beautiful one, and come along" (Song of Solomon 2:13).

She responded, "My beloved is mine and I am his" (Song of Solomon 2:16).

The kiss of *chashaq* had been planted, the kiss where no words need to be spoken, the deep, committed, I-love-you kiss.

The Shulammite's ridiculous request was answered when Solomon brought the young, beautiful virgin to his inner chamber and fervently placed on her lips the hot passionate kiss of *nasaq* (Song of Solomon 1:4). She became Solomon's wife, and the queen of Israel. She would reign with the king.

After seven days in the honeymoon suite, the couple came out into the real world. It is in the real world they must choose: Will they live "happily ever after" with blessings or will they choose curses?

Remaining in the Promised Land

After the Israelites passed through the cleavage of Mt. Ebal and Mt. Gerizim, they entered the promise land. It was an abundant land, a land flowing with milk and honey, a land with great prosperity and blessings. And it all belonged to them if they stayed in covenant with God. God warned the Israelites:

> See, I have set before you today life and prosperity, and death and adversity; in that I command you today to love the Lord your God, to walk in His ways and to keep His commandments and His statues and His judgments, that you may live and multiply, and that the Lord your God may bless you in the land where you are entering to possess it. But if your heart turns away and you will not obey, but are drawn away and worship other gods and serve them, I declare to you today that you shall surely perish. You shall not prolong your days in the land where you are crossing the Jordan to enter and possess it. I call heaven and earth to witness against you today, that I have set before you life and death, the blessing and the curse. So choose life in order that you may live, you and your descendants. (Deuteronomy 30:15-19)

It will be easy to put this book down and go about living your life as if nothing needs to change. After all, you've gotten by just fine living life according to your own standards. Who cares if you add a little extra time to your practice card in band so that you can receive the "A?" Your band teacher is never going to know. It doesn't hurt anyone when you cheat on a test, and besides you need good grades. Gossip is fun and girls are always going to do that, you rationalize. You're a prude if you aren't having sex or at least petting, and besides there's no harm in it. It's your personal business, right? If you want to live the rest of your life with blessings and not curses, you need to readjust your thinking and read on.

Staying in the Promised Land

As Solomon and his bride step out of the bridal chamber they are reminded of their covenant with each other and with God. They know from the history of the Israelites that if they want to rule with authority in the promised land they must follow three simple principles:

(1) They must **love** the LORD their God (Deuteronomy 30:20);
(2) They must **obey** His voice (Deuteronomy 30:20);
(3) They must **hold fast** to Him (Deuteronomy 30:20).

We Must Love the LORD Our God

Jesus told His disciples, "If you love Me, you will keep My commandments" (John 14:15). There are numerous commandments that God gave to His people in an outline form. He told His people:

(1) "You shall have no other gods before Me" (Exodus 20:3);
(2) "You shall not make for yourself an idol" (Exodus 20:4);
(3) "You shall not take the name of the LORD your God in vain" (Exodus 20:7);
(4) "Remember the Sabbath day, to keep it holy" (Exodus 20:7);
(5) "Honor your father and your mother" (Exodus 20:8);
(6) "You shall not murder" (Exodus 20: 13);
(7) "You shall not commit adultery" (Exodus 20:14);
(8) "You shall not steal" (Exodus 20:15);
(9) "You shall not bear false witness" (Exodus 20:16);
(10) "You shall not covet" (Exodus 20:17).

One of the Pharisees, a lawyer, asked Jesus, "Teacher, which is the greatest commandment in the Law?"

Jesus answered him, "You shall love the LORD your God with all your heart, and with all your soul, and with all you mind. This is the greatest and foremost commandment. The second is like it, you shall love your neighbor as yourself. On these two commandments depend the whole Law and the Prophets" (Matthew 22:35-40).

Loving God with All Our Heart

Jesus is telling us that if we love God with all of our hearts we will do the will of God. The Hebrew meaning of heart is the "will" and even "the intellect." The Bible tells us that God was looking and found a man after His own heart that would do His will (Acts 13:23). The man that God found was David, Solomon's father. David wasn't perfect by any stretch, but David served the purpose (will) of God in his own generation (Acts 13:36). Our first job in loving God is to ask the question: "What is God's will for my life?" The second step will be to circumcise our heart (cut away the flesh). So to love God with all our heart means to ask God what His will is for our lives, and then do His will and not the will of our own flesh.

Loving God with All of Our Mind

Secondly, Jesus is telling us that to love God with our minds means that we are to act and speak differently than the normal man. Mind in Greek means "intellect, understanding, will." As a verb it means, "can speak." In Hebrew it means "body, creature." Our minds tell our bodies what to do. Christ was the practical example for us. He showed us how to speak and act. We are fully capable of speaking and acting godly because we are to have the mind of Christ (1 Corinthians 2:16). Most of us don't act like Christ because we're focused on the fact that we are sinners; therefore, we act like sinners. However, the Bible tells us that while we were yet sinners Christ died for us how much more will He do for us now that we are righteous (Romans 5:8-9). It's time to throw the "W.W.J.D" (What Would Jesus Do) bracelets away and put on the "W.D J.D" (What Does Jesus Do) bracelets. He forgives people, He loves God, He thinks positive thoughts, and He loves you. Girls, if you know Jesus, you are righteous and have the mind of Christ. Speak and act in love, it will blow your friends away and tickle your heavenly Father to no end!

To love God with our minds is to speak and act on the Word of God.

Loving God with All of Our Soul

Thirdly, Jesus is telling us that to love God with our soul means that we have got to let the Holy Spirit work in us. *Psuche* (psoo-khay) is what the Greeks call the soul. It means, "breath, spirit, mind, superhuman, angel, Holy Spirit." In the Hebrew, soul means, "breath, refresh, wind, life, mind, and heart." Do you see how interconnected the heart, mind, and soul are? Yet they are all different. You could not live if one of them wasn't functioning. You cannot love if one of them is not functioning. One is not more important that the others.

If we are to love God with our souls, we have to learn to listen, obey and trust in the Holy Spirit, the breath of God. We need to stop leaning on our own understanding and stop being afraid of Its power. We let it take us over and work through us so that God can accomplish His will for our lives.

I picture Chevy Chase in the movie "Christmas Vacation" when he connects the strands of lights into one outlet. The whole house lights up as if it were a small city. That's what our lives will look like when we connect the power of the Holy Spirit, to the will of God, and the mind of Christ. We will act, speak, and perform amazing things. There is nothing that we can't accomplish and no one that we can't love if we first learn to love God with all our heart, mind, and soul. We wouldn't need to worry about any other commandment if we understood how to keep this ONE commandment!

What does this look like in our everyday life?

Let's pretend that you take great pride in the fact that you are the best athlete in the high school. Katie, a new girl, moves to the neighborhood and has taken the spotlight from you. Not only is she a better athlete, she's been voted most attractive female senior in the yearbook. You want to like her, but your pride and jealousy won't let you.

"Katie thinks she's so great," you remark to all your friends.

"She's really nice. I like her," your best friend replies.

"*I hate her*!" you screech inside.

You were taught in Sunday school that God's will is for you to love your neighbor (Katie) as yourself. But you choose to keep your pride and jealousy, and it is wearing you out, not to mention making you ugly.

The scripture "love your neighbor as yourself" keeps coming into your head. You keep telling yourself to be nice but as you see her in the hall your flesh screams out, *Trip her, spread gossip about her make her life miserable.*

You start asking the Holy Spirit to give you the power to act kindly to her and say nice things to her. When you do, something strange starts to happen to you. Your jealousy diminishes and you actually start talking to her in the hall and saying nice things about her. Your heart changes toward her and you begin to like her, all because you chose the will of God (to love her), spoke and acted as Christ did, and allowed the power of the Holy Spirit to change you from the inside out.

When we learn to love God with all our heart, mind, and soul, we will learn to love people with our mouths, actions, and emotions. We are going to have incredible, deep, meaningful relationships, not only with people but also with God.

Solomon knew how to love God. He did His will as he miraculously built a temple for God to dwell in (Solomon's temple). He spoke truth and love to the people that he reigned over. People were drawn to Solomon because of his relationship and love for God. "Now Solomon loved the Lord" (1 Kings 3:3).

If we want to reign in life we have to love God.

Obey His Voice

"Mom, you hear from God all the time. How do you know it's Him?" my daughter Jordan asked. "One way that God speaks to me is when I'm reading Scripture and the words just seem to jump of the page. It's as if I've never seen them before, but they are the answer I've been looking for. Another way that God speaks to me is when this very clear voice rings in my head. It puts a thought in my heart that I hadn't been thinking of and it never goes against scripture. It's profound and it's peaceful. It won't always make sense in the world's eyes but it will be very clear to you," I told her. "When you hear it, obey it."

My daughter, Jolene, and I nestled down near the front row of the beautiful church in Boulder, Colorado. She was a student at the University of Colorado and I was a visitor. I was in awe of all the well-dressed people. I didn't know that they existed in Boulder. I thought that to live in Boulder you must wear Birkenstock sandals and have your hair in dreadlocks. In the middle of my "awe" moment God said, "June, go outside and bring in the homeless bagger from the street corner."

"What!?" I said. "Lord, I will make a spectacle of myself if I get up now and go get him. What will these people think? I'm a guest in this church!"

"Go get him!" The strong voice commanded.

"Oh, boy," I muttered. I told my daughter I would be right back.

I got up from my comfortable pew and felt like everyone's eyes had zeroed in on my back as I made my way down the aisle and out the front door.

I looked to the right. No bum. I looked to the left. No bum. I sighed with relief. "He's not here."

"Look to your right again," the voice said.

Sure enough there was the homeless bagger that I had passed earlier on my way into the church. I cleared my throat and asked him, "Would you like to go to church with me?" Time froze for a moment. I hoped he would say "no."

"I would love to come," he replied.

"God, I don't know what you are doing but it better be good," I said to myself as I accompanied Steve down the aisle and into our pew.

My daughter and I took shallow breaths as the stench of Steve's body odor rolled over us, but I knew that it would be worth it. God was going to show up at any moment and heal Steve from his poverty. This church was about to be transformed. They were about to encounter God. I envisioned lightning bolts and an earthquake. *No better place for revival than Boulder*, I thought to myself. My hopes fell as I looked over my right shoulder; Steve had fallen to sleep right there in the pew. It wasn't an earthquake; just a lot of snoring.

The church service ended. Steve awoke and hurried out to the street corner where his cup might be filled with leftover tithes and offerings.

My daughter asked me on the way to the car, "What was that all about?"

"I don't know. I just know that I obeyed the voice of the Lord."

Solomon heard from God a second time. After Solomon finished building the house of the Lord, the Lord said to him:

> I have heard your prayer and your supplication, which you have made before Me; I have consecrated this house which you have built by putting My name there forever and My eyes and My heart will be there perpetually. As for you, if you will walk before Me as your father David walked in integrity of heart and uprightness, doing according to all that I have commanded you and will keep My statutes and My ordinance, then I will establish the throne of your kingdom over Israel forever, just as I promised to your father David, saying, 'You shall not lack a man on the throne of Israel.' But if you or your sons shall indeed turn away from following Me, and shall not keep My commandments and My statutes which I have set before you and shall go and serve other gods and worship them, then I will cut off Israel from the land which I have given them, and the house which I have consecrated for My name, I will cast out of My sight. So Israel will become a proverb and a byword among all peoples. And this house will become a heap of ruins; everyone who passes by will be astonished and hiss and say, 'Why has the Lord done thus to this land and to this house?' And they will say, 'Because they forsook the Lord their God, who brought

> their fathers out of the land of Egypt, and adopted other gods and worshiped them and served them, therefore the Lord has brought all this adversity on them.'" (1 Kings 9:1-9)

When God tells us to do something He expects us to do it. Solomon was very aware of this because he knew that God's voice commanded a king to rise above the rest. Kings were required to do things that commoners weren't, and God made four things very clear to Solomon: ". . . he wasn't to multiply horses for himself, he wasn't to multiply wives for himself . . . (or else his heart would turn away), he wasn't to . . . greatly increase silver and gold for himself, and he was to copy God's laws on a scroll in the presence of the Levitical priests" (Deuteronomy 17:16-18). He had to obey and not change one jot or tittle if he was to stay in the promised land.

If we want to rule, reign, and stay in our promised land we must obey God's voice, even when it doesn't make sense to us.

Hold Fast to God

Last, but not least, if we are going to stay in the promised land we have to learn to hold fast to God (Deuteronomy 30:20). The New King James translation says, "To cleave" to. It means, "to cling to, be joined together."

Imagine yourself in a raging river, there is a huge waterfall the size of Niagara Falls at the end. You can't get out because the sides are steep and the water is too swift. Frantically you try to swim upstream but lose hope, when all of a sudden you see a large tree with its branches hanging over the water's edge. You grab hold of the branch, knowing that it is your only hope for survival. This is how God wants us to hold fast to Him, knowing that we have to cling to him and not let go because if we do will be swept away in the current.

God doesn't want Solomon and his new bride to depend on anyone or anything other than Him (Proverbs 3:5).

If we want to rule and reign in our promised land, we must hold fast to God.

The Test

Our love for God, our obedience, and our faith or lack thereof it, along with Solomon's, is going to be evident as God gives us pop quizzes to see if we trust Him. When we pass the small tests, He's going to give us bigger ones.

These tests aren't for the Lord to see where our hearts are; they are for us to see where our hearts are. They are a test to see if we are more in love with the Promiser or the promised land. Are we more in love with the Promiser or the promises?

The prophet Jeremiah said, "Thus says the Lord, cursed is the man who trusts in mankind and makes flesh his strength, and whose heart turns away from the Lord . . . blessed is the man who trusts in the Lord and whose trust is the Lord" (Jeremiah 17:5, Jeremiah 17:7).

God tested Noah for 100 years to see if he was committed and would be obedient to build the ark. He tested Abraham to see if he loved Him more than Isaac. He tested the Israelites to see if they would believe in His promises. They failed when they wouldn't enter the promised land the first time because of fear but were later tested and passed, thus entering into the promised land.

While blow-drying my hair one day the Lord began to show me a video in my head of a test that I had passed. He spoke to me so kindly, "June, do you remember the bagger, Steve, that you encountered a few years ago?"

"How could I forget?" I responded.

"That was a test! You passed. I have much to entrust to you."

I wept, I love you, Lord!"

When we start passing the tests in our lives, the King of the universe will show us how much we love and trust Him. He will begin to entrust territories (ministries, organizations, communities) to us so that we might rule and reign over them as queen.

Your pop quiz might be a simple test in honesty. Will you cheat on the test? He could quiz you on relationships. If you're lonely, will you grab the first friend that comes by or will you wait on the Lord? How about your future husband? Will you trust God to provide him, or will you go through many broken relationships to try and find him?

God has given me many quizzes. Some I failed miserably and some I passed with flying colors, but one particular test changed the course of my life.

When Jay and I first moved to Grand Junction, we were living in an apartment close to Mesa State College that barely had running water. We only had one car, so I would walk to the grocery store with my six-month-old baby, purchase a limited amount of groceries, and then borrow their shopping cart to take my groceries home. I looked like a homeless bag lady.

None of this seemed to affect Jay. He had dreams, goals, and ambitions. That's why he became a REALTOR. There was one problem: commissions. You don't make any money unless you actually sell real estate. You don't sell real estate if you don't have clients. You don't have clients when you are new to a city.

I desperately needed a job to make ends meet. I found an OB-GYN looking for a medical secretary and bookkeeper in the help-wanted ads, so I went in for an interview.

"So, June, do you have any experience in this field?" the doctor asked.

"Well, I know how to balance my checkbook and I did take bookkeeping in high school," I said.

"I perform abortions in this office. How do you feel about that?"

I don't know how I feel about abortions, I thought. *No one ever talked about it where I came from.* But something inside of me knew that they were wrong.

Wanting to be politically correct, I answered, "Doesn't everyone have the right to choose?"

I went home that night realizing that I had to be the least qualified person for the job, but something inside of me knew I was going to get it. Sure enough, the next day I received the call and went to work immediately.

I loved this job. The doctor was very good to me and even offered to pay me if I would stay after hours and clean the office. I agreed and began my new janitorial services. Night after night I cleaned alone, always saving the "abortion room" until last. There was an eerie feeling, a darkness that covered this room. I couldn't wait to get out of it.

Work during the day was business as usual until one day the nurse came up from the back room crying. She asked for my help. "June, one of the patients just aborted ten-week-old twin fetuses. Could you help me piece them back together?"

By law, the nurse had to make sure that every part of the fetus was out of the mother's womb because if there was any tissue left in the mother, she could bleed to death.

Nothing could have prepared me for what I was about to see. There, lying in a Petri dish, were two perfectly formed babies. Their little arms had been ripped away from their bodies. Their little hands had five fingers and their feet had five toes, all of which had been ripped apart by the abortionist. There they lay motionless, as we, by law, pieced them back together.

My heart sank. I began to cry. *Oh, God, forgive me for being so stupid.* I had thought a fetus was just a mass of blood and tissue until way late in the pregnancy. I didn't realize that these babies were fully formed.

I confessed. "Lord, I set up their appointments. I've been an accomplice to these crimes. Please forgive me."

I needed this job. I loved this job. But I knew it wasn't right. I handed in my resignation and prayed God would provide another job quickly. He answered and provided a job at a bank; a job that I hated.

After three months on the job, I found myself pregnant with our second child. Our finances hadn't gotten any better. I was miserable and mad at God because, out of obedience to Him, I had given up a job that I loved and was put in a job that I hated. I desperately wanted to stay home and raise my own kids, but I had no choice. I had to work. I remember going to lunch by myself and just sitting at the table crying. I'm sure the waitress thought someone had died.

I bowed my head at that restaurant table and said to God, "I realize how precious life is to You. I know how much You love kids and I know that You've given these babies to me, not some day-care to raise. I want to be their mother. I want to stay home full time and raise them. But it's Christmas, Lord. We have no money, we've bought no gifts, and more than anything I just want to go back to my hometown and be with my family for the holidays."

"June, go quit your job!" the Lord said.

"When, Lord?" I whispered.

"Now?"

"But, God," I said, "It's Christmas. We have no money, no gifts, and my husband doesn't have any contracts!"

God said, "Do you trust me?"

"Yes, Lord."

"I will be your provider. You will not want. Now go quit your job!"

My flesh was waging war against me. *Don't quit, you idiot.* God was testing me. "Do you love me? Will you obey Me? Will you hold fast to Me?" In the world's eyes, it was nonsense to quit my job. But was I going to live by God-sense or nonsense?

I went to my boss and stood before her. "I've come to tell you that I'm quitting."

She said, "Are you giving your two weeks' notice?"

"No." I said. *What was I to tell her? God and I were having lunch and He told me to quit today?*

"I'm not coming back after today," I stated quietly.

"Does your husband know?"

"No," I said, wondering why she had asked. As I stood there, she called the president of the bank and told him that I had quit.

He asked her, "Does her husband know?"

She said, "No, her husband doesn't know."

Who are these people I thought to myself, *and why do they keep asking if my husband knows?*

What I didn't know is that my husband was sitting outside the president's door waiting to have a meeting with him. *Of all the days! Didn't God know that I was quitting at 5:00 p.m.? Why was my husband there?*

God had ordained the whole meeting. Jay was there to sell the president of the bank an ad for a home magazine. He would sell him the whole back cover and make eight hundred dollars that very night.

From the very moment I trusted and obeyed the voice of God, He began to work miracles in our lives. Jay's business has flourished and I've been a stay-at-home mom ever since. God has provided more than I ever dreamed of. You see, I no longer live in the mortuary, listening to the prince of this world. I live in covenant with the Prince of Peace, the Prince who has promised to provide for me, protect me, and give me great pleasure. He loves me! Now when God tells us to do something, I guarantee that there will be a few pop quizzes and then a test to see where our hearts are. Do we love and trust in God? Or do we trust in ourselves or other men?

The Testing of Solomon

The Guttenberg press hasn't been invented; therefore, it is the king's job to make a copy of the law, "the law of Moses" (Deuteronomy 17:18). Solomon is to copy the law in front of the priest so that not one jot or tittle, not one period, comma, or letter is changed. No one has authority to change the law, not even Jesus (Matthew 5:17-18). Solomon is to make sure that the covenant is correctly passed down to the next generation so that they will know how to live their lives with blessings.

Here's the test. Will Solomon write the law word for word, jot for jot, tittle for tittle, or will he, in his great wisdom have a better plan?

The words that the King is supposed to be transcribing are ". . . He shall not multiply wives for himself, or else his heart will turn away" (Deuteronomy 17:17). According to the Jewish teaching called the Midrash Rabbah, Solomon erased a *yod* a little letter from the word "multiply" (*yirbeh*). The *yod* is a letter shaped like an apostrophe and no larger than one. It is just a small jot of ink. By erasing the letter *yod*, Solomon has changed the tense of the verb "multiply." It is a small but subtle change. But now the verse is no longer an imperative forbidding a king to multiply wives. Instead, it has become a statement implying that his past-tense multiplication of wives will not have the effect of leading his heart astray.[4]

With his wisdom Solomon reasoned that God gave this command so that His heart wouldn't be turned from God. As long as he kept his heart right he could have multiple wives (Midrash Rabbah). Having multiple wives was socially acceptable; in fact, it made a lot of sense politically. Marrying princesses from other nations was a security move. If you married the daughter of a neighboring kingdom; chances were you would have the king as your ally. Solomon not only disobeyed God, but didn't trust him either.

With one erased *yod*, Solomon becomes directionally dysfunctional. His moral compass becomes obscured because he trades in his God-sense for nonsense (worldly ways).

> King Solomon loved many foreign woman along with the daughter of Pharaoh; Moabite, Ammonite, Edomite, Sidonian, and Hittite women, from the nations concerning which the Lord had said to the sons of Israel, you shall not associate with them, neither shall they associate with you, for they will surely turn your heart away after their gods, Solomon held fast to these in love" (1 Kings 11:1-2).
>
> "Solomon acquired seven hundred wives, princesses, and three hundred concubines, and his wives turned his heart away" (1Kings 11:3).

Now before we throw our hands up and get mad at Solomon we need to see how we do the very thing that Solomon did. We change the Word of God to fit our lifestyle. We also rationalize that in college it's easier to live with one guy than fight with multiple girl roommates, and economically it makes sense to share a house or apartment because one day we are going to get married.

We change the law that says, "Thou shall not commit adultery" (Exodus 20:14). We think we know the intent of the law. So we change it a little and say it is okay as long as someday we get married.

In all his wisdom Solomon thinks he understands the reasoning behind God's commandment. As long as his heart isn't turned from God, he can have multiple wives. But in all of his wisdom he doesn't understand the strengths of

---

4 *Restoration* D. Thomas Lancaster

a woman. He has no idea that God has created the woman in such a unique way that she has the power to move the hearts of kings.

Eve moved the heart of Adam, and sin entered the world. Delilah moved the heart of Sampson and the Philistines seized him and gouged out his eyes. Esther moved the heart of King Ahasuerus and saved a Jewish nation. Sari moved the heart of Abram and a nation was born that would always cause problems for God's people. Mary captured the heart of God and a Savior was brought into the world.

It was a woman named Madelyn Murray O'Hair that moved the hearts of judges and removed prayer from schools. Norma McCorvey, better known as Jane Roe, moved the hearts of judges to legalize the killing of unborn babies.

As a young woman do not underestimate your strengths and your role in God's kingdom. If you want to rule in the promised land you have to love God, obey His voice and hold fast to Him.

You will be the next generation of women that will turn the heads and hearts of men. So turn them toward Christ.

While getting ready to teach my last lesson of "*Wake Up, Sleeping Beauty*" to a group of high school girls, I went before the Lord and I asked Him, "Lord is there anything else that you want to tell these girls?"

He replied, "Tell them how much I love them!"

Sweet, young, beautiful, virgin girls, Jesus loves you so much that He died for you. Will you wake up and live for him? Will you trade in your non-sense for God-sense?

Sleeping Beauty knew the key to living "happily ever after." Accept the kiss from your "True Love" (Jesus) and follow the ways of His kingdom.

Have you accepted "true love's kiss" (God's truth), His *Ketubah* to you?

God gives you the key to living "happily ever after." "Today I have put before you life [living God's way] and death [living our lives according to the world], the blessing and the curse. So choose life" (Deuteronomy 30:19). Amen.

Kingdom Challenge:

Do you remember when I told you that the scariest moment of my life was when I would have to close down the mortuary for the night? I was so afraid that the dead person in the casket might open his eyes and come back to life.

Satan has the very same fear. He comes to close you in at night and hopes that you have not received your "true love's kiss." It's time to scare the heebie-jeebies out of Satan. It's time to receive God's truth, open your eyes, and get out of the casket. It's time to shake the dust from you and rise up. You are going to loosen the chains from your neck: no more bitterness, anger, self-pity, and sexual sins for you. You are going to leave the mortuary and start living for the Lord. You are going to get involved in your church and in your community. "For the Lord will go before you and the God of Israel will be your rear guard" (Isaiah 52: 1-2, 11-12). It's time to *Wake Up, Sleeping Beauty* and change the hearts of kings.

Your final challenge is to set your standards high! Girls, when you stop dating guys who lie, cheat, want premarital sex, are lazy, and treat you poorly, you will start meeting guys who will raise their standards to yours!

Today's One-liner:..................................Jesus (The Word) is True Love's Kiss
Clue for living "Happily Ever After":............................... Deuteronomy 30:19

> *"Today I have put before you life and death the blessing and the curse. So choose life."*

Kiss of Love:.. Life
Kiss of Betrayal:...Death